MR CROOK'S CRIME ACADEMY

SAFE-CRACKING FOR STUDENTS

A BOOK THIS FUNNY SHOULD BE AGAINST THE LAW!

FROM THE BEST-SELLING AUTHOR OF HORRIBLE HISTORIES™

TERRY DEARY

Illustrated by John Kelly

■SCHOLASTIC

Scholastic Children's Books
An imprint of Scholastic Ltd
Euston House, 24 Eversholt Street
London, NW1 1DB, UK
Registered office: Westfield Road, Southam, Warwickshire, CV47 0RA
SCHOLASTIC and associated logos are trademarks and/or registered trademarks
of Scholastic Inc.

First published in the UK by Scholastic Ltd, 2010
This edition published 2010

Text copyright © Terry Deary, 2010
Illustration copyright © John Kelly, 2010

The right of Terry Deary and John Kelly to be identified as the author
and illustrator of this work has been asserted by them.

Cover illustration © John Kelly, 2010

ISBN 978 1 407 12448 3

Printed by CPI Bookmarque, Croydon
Papers used by Scholastic Children's Books are made from wood grown in
sustainable forests.

1 3 5 7 9 10 8 6 4 2

www.scholastic.co.uk/zone

CONTENTS

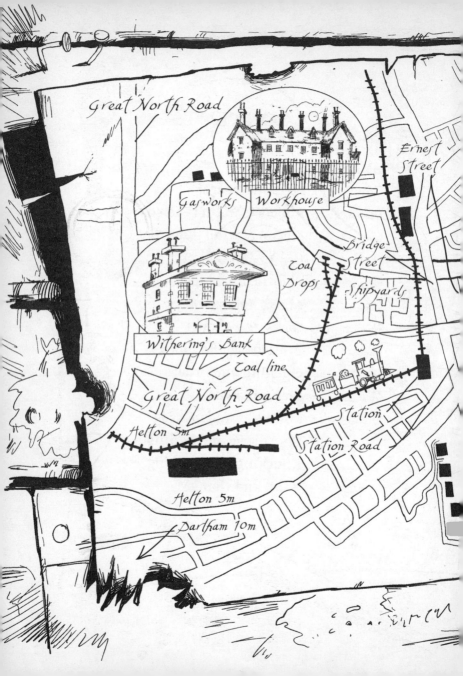

Before word

If crimes were mountains then bank robbery would be Mount Everest.

Some people gaze out of the window when they should be listening to their Geography teacher. If you are one of those people then you probably DON'T know Mount Everest is the world's highest mountain. Some of you will KNOW that. If you already know then why are you reading this note, eh? Stop wasting time and get on with the tale.

Bank robbery is top of the tree, pick of the pile and best of the bestest. It is the greatest work of art since William Shakespeare gave up painting.

Sadly, there is a little country on the other side of the Atlantic called the United States of America. In the US of A they do not treat bank robbery as an art, the way we do.

There are these terribly rough chaps called "cowboys" – maybe because they are half cow and half man – and they carry guns. They walk into a bank, they shoot a few people, they steal some money and they ride off . . . probably on a cow.

Police officers called "sheriffs" ride after them, catch

them and take them back to town to be hanged.

One of the most famous cowboys was Billy the Kid. Now, as you know, a kid is a small goat. So Billy the Kid must have been Billy the Goat. Maybe he was half goat and half man.

They say he had "buck teeth". A buck is a rabbit . . . so perhaps I'm wrong. Perhaps he was half rabbit and half goat.

His wanted poster must have been a beauty!

WANTED

BILLY THE KID
OUTLAW
DEAD OR ALIVE

Now, where was I? Oh, yes, US bank robbers. Boring.

British bank robbers? That's a different story. British bank robbers were men of skill. No one was hurt . . . nothing was hurt, except the pockets of the rich.

One of the most daring bank robberies took place in the little northern town of Wildpool. Wildpool has been described as a "poor little, muddy little, cold little, wind-wracked, wave-washed, smoke-choked, rat-riddled, sour-smelling little town."

I should know. I was the one who described it that way. People of Wildpool do not LIKE reading that about their town. "It's a lovely place," they splutter angrily. "Aha," I reply. "I am writing about the Wildpool of over sixty years ago. I was there — you weren't. Believe me, it was as grim and grimy as a tramp's socks."

As well as the tale of a wonderful bank robbery Wildpool had another strange tale to tell. The tale of a school that was set up just to teach young people how to break the law . . . and not get caught. Don't you wish YOU went to a school like that?

In Wildpool you COULD. It was called Master Crook's Crime Academy and this is one of its great tales.

I was there and gathered the facts from the robbers.

If you want to witness the wonder of Wildpool then read on.

If you want a tale of guns, hangings and kids that are boy-cows then go to the US of A.

Mr X

23 April 1901

Chapter 1

SIGN AND SECRET

Wildpool Town – Monday 3rd April 1837

It took three men to put up the sign. It was a large sign painted in red with gold lettering.

They dug two holes, placed a post in each hole and then heaved them upright.

The men didn't know they were being watched. Across the road was an old house. The house had a sign outside its door too.

MASTER CROOK'S CRIME ACADEMY

Tuition for the children of the poor to help them stay out of prison.

Five pupils stood at the window of an upstairs classroom and watched the men across the High Street. The pupils were in the top class of Master Crook's Crime Academy.

They were also in the bottom class.

"How is that?" (you gasp in amazement). I will tell you. They were the only class.

Master Crook kept school records, of course. The records for the class of April 1837 looked like this:

MASTER CROOK'S CRIME ACADEMY

Name: **Smiff Smith**

Registered: **January 1837**

Teacher's comment: **Shoplifter. Could turn out to be a top criminal. Keen to learn and good at talking his way out of trouble.**

MASTER CROOK'S CRIME ACADEMY

Name: Alice White

Registered: January 1837

Teacher's comment: Match girl and beggar. Bad-tempered and wild but has a lot of common sense and a kind heart (under that fierce scowl).

MASTER CROOK'S CRIME ACADEMY

Name: Nancy Turnip

Registered: February 1837

Teacher's comment: Serving maid. A quiet and nervous girl but very determined to rob the rich and help the poor. Strong as a carthorse, gentle as a lamb.

MASTER CROOK'S
CRIME ACADEMY

Name: Martin Mixly

Registered: February 1837

Teacher's comment: Schoolboy. Looks like a quiet, honest boy but that's an act. Determined to make the rich pay for their crimes. Bright as a button.

MASTER CROOK'S
CRIME ACADEMY

Name: Millie Mixly

Registered: February 1837

Teacher's comment: Martin's twin. Quick-thinking and brave as a lion. Always ready to help someone in trouble.

"It's a prison! They're building a prison," Millie Mixly breathed, watching the men across the High

Street. "They're going to lock us all away if we get caught."

"Who says? You says?" Alice White snorted. "There's a perfectly bad gaol in Darlham. There's not enough crime in Wildpool to have a prison. Anyway . . . we're not going to get caught, Millie Mixly. Not unless you're really stupid . . . like Smiff Smith!"

Smiff sniffed . . . sort of smiffed. He wasn't going to let Alice upset him. "You can't tell what it'll be till it's finished. They've only built the ground floor so far. Why do you think it's a prison, Millie?" he asked.

"All the windows have thick bars across them," she explained. "To keep people in."

"Sometimes bars are used to keep people out," Nancy said quietly. "When I worked for Mayor Twistle he had iron bars on his wine cellar to keep the servants out."

"Did it work?" Martin Mixly asked.

"No. He gave the key to the butler every time he wanted wine. The butler had a copy made. We could get in any time we liked."

The pupils nodded. Sometimes the rich and greedy could be very stupid. The classroom door opened. A man walked in. He wore a shabby top hat and a

red-and-white striped scarf around his neck. His gooseberry-green eyes bulged like a bulldog's. His fingers were thin and they rippled when he talked.

"Good morning, class, and what a fine spring morning it is too." The class kept their eyes fixed on the workmen as they struggled to raise the sign that would be nailed to the boards. The man sighed. "And good morning to *you*, Mr Dreep. Yes, it is a fine day," he said to himself.

Alice White turned. "Oh, it's you, Mr Dreep."

"What a pleasant way to greet your teacher. You have the manners of a farmyard goat, Alice."

"Oh, sir!" Smiff cried. "That's a rotten thing to say about a goat."

Alice looked as if she wanted to butt the boy. Butt she didn't.

"Please, Mr Dreep," Nancy said quickly, "can you tell us what they are building across the road?"

The teacher nodded. "Master Crook tells me it is something we have always dreamed of!"

"I dream of pushing Smiff off a cliff," Alice said, suddenly sweet.

"I just dream of Alice losing her voice," the boy said.

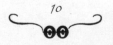

"Look," the teacher said, "the sign is going up now."

The men pushed and struggled and wobbled and wibbled. But at last the sign was raised in front of the half-finished building.

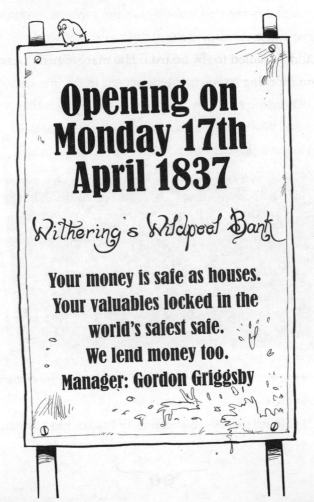

Opening on Monday 17th April 1837

Withering's Wildpool Bank

**Your money is safe as houses.
Your valuables locked in the world's safest safe.
We lend money too.
Manager: Gordon Griggsby**

"A bank!" Martin cried. "Oh that's perfect!"

"We don't have to burgle fifty rich houses . . . we just let them bring their stuff to the bank and we take it all at once," Millie agreed.

"We've never had lessons in bank robbery," Nancy said quietly. "Who will teach us?"

Samuel Dreep took off his hat and scarf and placed them on a hat-stand by the door.

"There are two ways to rob a bank," the teacher told the class as they scrambled to sit at their desks.

He wrote on the blackboard with a stick of chalk:

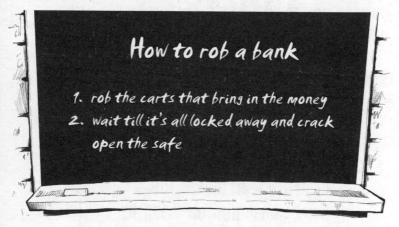

How to rob a bank

1. rob the carts that bring in the money
2. wait till it's all locked away and crack open the safe

"Which will we do?" Smiff asked.

Mr Dreep's eyes glowed like Wildpool gas lamps.

"Both," he said. "We'll try both."

Wildpool police station stood next to Master Crook's Crime Academy. Constable Septimus Liddle (PC 01) and Constable Archibald Larch (PC 02) sat in their room. Constable Liddle was thin as a drainpipe and his wispy, white moustache drooped sadly.

Constable Larch opened the newspaper to look at the horse-racing results. His round, red face was as gloomy as doom. "Oh, dear," he sighed. "Lost again. I've never seen one of my horses win."

"No . . . funny that . . . you never see one of your *horses* win. But you see invisible dogs!" Liddle sniggered.

Larch glared. "Don't mention invisible dogs. You promised not to mention them ever again."

"Sorry, Larch." Liddle was polishing his top hat. He looked over the top of the hat to the front page of the newspaper. "Oh, dear, oh dear, oh dear! A dead policeman!"

Constable Larch's piggy eyes peered, squinted and almost disappeared into the folds of fat in his cheeks. "Where? I can't smell no dead policeman!"

"On the front of your newspaper!" Liddle cried.

"There's a dead policeman on the front of my newspaper? How did he get there?"

"No, no, no . . . there's a *report* about a dead policeman. Who is it, Larch?"

"How would I know? It's not you and it's not me . . . though I sometimes wonder about you, Septimus," the lardy lawman said. "Let's have a look," he muttered, turning the newspaper.

3 April 1837

THE WILDPOOL BUGLE

CONSTABLE DEAD

He read slowly. "We are sad to announce that John Constable has died in London at the age of sixty-one. Mr Constable was famous for his painting."

"Aw! That's nice. A policeman that paints. He could come round to my house!" Liddle said.

"Why's that?"

"Well, my house needs a lick of paint."

"I don't think he's that sort of painter," Larch said, frowning. "I think he paints pictures."

"Oh, a policeman that paints *pictures*. Nice. I could do that. What did he die from? Was he attacked while he was on duty?"

"It says here he had an attack of indigestion. I get that very bad myself. Especially after I've eaten one of Mrs Bunton's meat pies. Ah, it says Mr Constable is famous for painting Salisbury Cathedral!"

"I thought you said he didn't paint houses? If he painted a cathedral he could paint a house. Big things is cathedrals. He must have had very long ladders!"

John Constable WAS famous for painting pictures, as you probably know. But Liddle makes a good point. What did Mr Constable do when Mrs Constable said, "The house needs painting, John"? Did he pay a house painter to do it? Did he give the man a free painting. Or did he get out a bucket of paint and do it himself? It is one of the great mysteries of life. Someone should ask him. I suppose him being dead is a problem though.

"And he's famous for painting a cornfield," Larch gasped.

"A cornfield! He must have used a hell of a big brush," Liddle said.

"Language, Liddle."

"Sorry, Larch. But he was a busy man. Where did he find the time? I mean we have a full-time job being constables. We couldn't fit in painting a cathedral."

"We wouldn't have to," his portly partner said. "There aren't any cathedrals in Wildpool."

Constable Liddle blew out his thin cheeks. "I'm pleased about that. I mean. I'm nearly sixty-one myself. If I had to run up and down ladders painting cathedrals I'd probably drop dead too. This job's hard enough."

"What job?" came a deep voice from the doorway.

Liddle and Larch jumped to their feet, jammed their top hats on their heads, and saluted. "Mornin' all!" they said.

""What job is hard enough?" said the man in a black suit. He was so enormous he made large Larch look like a puppy.

"Oh, Inspector Beadle," Larch said, "we were just

reading about this constable that died in London. He was attacked by indigestion. We were just saying what a hard job it is being a constable."

The inspector walked into the office and the floorboards creaked. "John Constable was a famous painter. He wasn't a policeman," he explained.

Liddle gave a slim smile. "That's how he had time to paint cathedrals then," he nodded.

"And you have time to paint cathedrals too. You could do it while you're sitting here in the police station," Beadle growled.

"No, sir," Larch said, shaking his head till his chins wobbled. "There's no cathedral in Wildpool."

"And we haven't any ladders long enough," Liddle added.

Inspector Beadle closed his eyes and counted slowly to ten. His fists were so tight the knuckles turned white. At last he said, "I have a special job for you two. A job so secret you must tell no one. No one at all."

"I can't even tell Liddle?" Larch asked.

"Liddle will know," the inspector sighed.

"So it's not a secret!" Larch said.

"Liddle will know because I will tell you both," the

inspector said. He rolled his eyes. "Sometimes I worry about crime in Wildpool," he muttered.

"It's all right, Inspector, sir," Liddle said. "Like Mayor Twistle said, we'll carry our truncheons like flaming torches of justice. We will bring light to the darkness of our savage streets."

"Sometimes you have to stay in the dark," Inspector Beadle said and tapped his nose in a wise way. "And I am sending you somewhere very, very dark. I will explain when you get back from your morning patrol."

Liddle and Larch left the police station and blinked in the early spring sunshine. "I hope we don't get attacked by any of those nasty indigestions like that London constable," Liddle said and his wispy moustache, thin as parsnip soup, trembled at the thought.

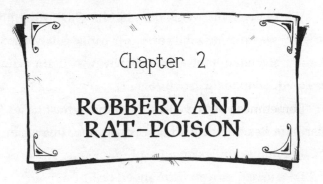

Chapter 2

ROBBERY AND
RAT-POISON

The manager of Withering's bank stood and watched the men heave the sign into place. Gordon Griggsby was a round sort of man. He had a round, shining head on a round body that was bursting the buttons on his black suit. Even his legs looked like two balls balanced on top of one another and the round toe-caps of his black boots made his feet look round too.

Except the soles and heels of the boots. They were flat. Flat as the Earth . . . otherwise he'd have had trouble walking, wouldn't he?

Once he was satisfied the sign was in place, Gordon

Griggsby turned and walked the short distance across the High Street to Master Crook's Crime Academy.

"Who's that man? What does he want? Do you think he knows we plan to rob the bank?" Millie Mixly cried as she watched him turn into the driveway of the school and waddle up to the front door.

"He'll tell the police! They'll come to arrest us all," Martin moaned. "We'll all be hanged. We'll swing in the breeze like apples on a tree."

"Like *what*?" Alice White sneered.

"Apples! It's a figure of speech."

"Core," she said with a wicked smile.

"You won't be laughing when you're on the gallows."

"No, I won't be laughing. I'll be too busy swinging like an apple," she agreed.

Gordon Griggsby's fist was as round as a ball and it bounced against the red front door.

"I'll get it," Nancy Turnip said. She'd been a maid-servant for years and she was used to answering doors. The girl hurried downstairs and tugged the door open.

Gordon Griggsby smiled at her as she bobbed

down in a curtsey. "Good afternoon, sir," she said. "Whom do you wish to see?"

"Well, this is Master Crook's academy so I hoped I would catch Master Crook himself."

"Sorry, sir, Master Crook never sees anyone . . . and no one sees him," the girl said.

"Are you a pupil here?"

"Please, sir, yes sir," Nancy said carefully.

"Then you have a teacher?"

"Oh!" she smiled and her pale moon face turned bright.

When I say "moon" face I mean a full moon . . . round and white. I don't mean a new moon or a half moon. If she had a half-moon face she'd have had half a face, wouldn't she? One eye, one ear, half a nose and half a chin. She would also have half a brain . . . just like anyone who thought I meant half-moon.

"We have Mr Samuel Dreep to teach us."

"A man with curly side whiskers, a top hat and a red-and-white scarf? I just saw him come in here. Perhaps I could have a word with Mr Dreep."

"Who should I say is calling, sir?" Nancy asked politely.

"Gordon Griggsby, the manager of Withering's bank."

"I'll fetch him, sir. We're just in the middle of a lesson."

"No, I'll come to the classroom. I want to see you all," Gordon Griggsby said and stepped inside the house, closing the door behind him. Nancy felt suddenly trapped as the man's round body blocked the way out and the door shut out the light.

"Upstairs, sir," she said and led the way.

The stairs creaked and wheezed, and so did Gordon Griggsby, as he climbed. "So what lesson is it today?" he asked.

"Errrr . . . banks and locks!"

"River banks and Scottish lochs, eh? Geography, then?"

"If you say so, sir."

They entered the classroom. Three pupils sat at their desks, their faces frozen and the itch of the hangman's rope felt around each neck. Smiff was standing at the blackboard with a cloth ready to wipe

it but stopped with the cloth in his hand. He used it to wipe his nose instead.

Please don't try this in school. It makes a snotty smudge on the board and when the teacher comes to write over it the chalk makes a horrible screech. It also leaves chalk on your nose. If you HAVE to wipe your nose then use your sleeve like everybody else.

"This is Mr Griggsby, the bank manager," Nancy announced to the class.

Samuel Dreep stepped forward to meet the man. He stretched out his fine fingers, as thin as October ice, to shake the round hand of the bank manager.

"Welcome, Mr Griggsby. I am so pleased to see you. The class are all great admirers of banks and money, and of course of Wildpool's wonderful police force. There could hardly be better men to guard the riches of the town. What can we do for you?"

Gordon Griggsby turned and let his twinkling dark eyes look over the five frightened faces.

"I understand you are a Crime Academy?"

"So what?" Alice said.

"So, you are learning how to fight crime, are you not?"

Alice felt the air rush out of her as if she'd been holding her breath for five minutes . . . which she probably had. "Yeah, that's right."

"One day you will take the place of the great constables Liddle and Larch?" Gordon Griggsby asked.

"Right," Smiff Smith nodded.

"So, today, I am here to give you the chance to take part in a little experiment," the bank manager went on. He smiled at Martin Mixly. "You will have seen they are building a bank across the road."

"Are they?" Martin gasped. "I never knew that. Did you know that, Millie?"

"No, Martin. I never guessed. Fancy that. Goodness me. How amazing. I never knew."

"That's two never knew," Martin said. "Did you knew, Smiff?"

"I never knew."

"Did you knew, Nancy?"

"I never knew."

"Did you knew, Alice?"

"Oh shut up, Martin. The bank manager isn't

stupid. He knows we know and I know he knows we know and I'll bet he knows I know he knows we know. Isn't that right, sir?"

"I think so," the bank manager said. "But my point is, the bank is always a magnet for criminals."

"Only if the criminals are made of scrap iron," Alice argued. "Don't tell me, it's a figure of speech?"

"I mean . . . criminals from all over the north will come to see if they can rob the riches inside. Now there are two ways to rob a bank," the bank manager went on.

"You can rob the carts that bring in the money . . . or you wait till it's all locked away and crack open the safe." Alice nodded. "We know that," she said glancing at the blackboard.

"Good!" the bank manager chuckled while his round head bobbed back and forth. "That means you can help the Wildpool police force. We need people we can trust for a very special job."

"What do you want us to do?" Millie Mixly asked.

Gordon Griggsby spread his round hands. "Why, I want you to rob a cart that is bringing in the money!"

The class were stunned. They were speechless. They could not find the words to even say how

shocked they were. So they said, ". . .!"

A house near Darlham – Monday 3rd April 1837

The man was not tall but he seemed to fill the fine
room. His dark brown hair was swept back from his
forehead and hung, too long, over his bone-white,
starched-hard, sharp-edged collar. His eyebrows hung
like curtains over his eyes and his beard was cut as
square and heavy as a church door.

His back was to the fire which crackled and
warmed the rich room, with chairs of violet velvet
and carpets of white wool, that was lit with the greeny
glow of gas lights. They sparkled on the wine-and-
white woven wallpaper, the crystal clock on the
marble mantelshelf, the cheerful china figures in clear
cases and on the portraits that peered at you from
glittering gold frames.

A girl watched him from the table where she
played with a large dolls' house. "I don't want this
dolls' house any longer," she said.

"Too old for dolls, my cherub?" the man asked.

"No. I mean I want a *palace* not a house. I want it
covered with gold and lit by lanterns with windows

made of rubies and diamonds, emeralds and sapphires."

The woman in the corner of the room kept her head down over her embroidery and her fingers fluttered like butterfly wings. "Oh, Charlotte!" she breathed. "We mustn't be greedy. Your father is a rich man but he isn't a prince. And I'm not sure you deserve a new toy after what went on at your school."

The girl gave her mother a glare hot enough to peel paint from a lamp post. "You can buy me a golden palace, can't you, Daddy?"

The man's moustache moved as if he were smiling behind the beard. "There are people out there who want to take our money from us, Lottie. Today I could buy us *all* a palace covered in gold. Tomorrow we could be robbed of every penny."

Charlotte scowled. "I like my money, Daddy. I don't want to lose it," she said fiercely. Her pink satin dress rustled like a snake's dead skin and her ringlets trembled with rage.

"Your money?" her mother said and gave a soft laugh. "It's your *father's* money, my dear."

"When he dies it will be mine," Charlotte said with a shrug. "The Sharkle fortune will be all mine . . .

28

when you and Daddy are dead and in the Sharkle tomb. And *no one* is going to steal it from *me*."

The man chuckled. "That is why we are putting money towards building Withering's bank in Wildpool. It will have the safest safe in the strongest strong-room. The inspector of police is a man called Beadle. He has told me his wonderful Wildpool police force will make sure no thieving thugs get within a mile of our hordes of treasure. Never fear, Lottie my lovely. The bank manager, Mr Griggsby, has even arranged a test to show the world how safe our fortune is."

"Show the world?" the girl said sharply. "What does that mean?"

"It means, little Lottie, that any Wildpool villains are welcome to watch and see how we deal with robbers."

Charlotte Sharkle lifted a wooden doll from the house. It was dressed like a serving man in a perfect little black suit and white shirt and tiny leather shoes. "Ooooh, dear, Mr Wildpool villain," she said to the doll. "I think you stole my missing watch. How do you plead?"

The girl held the doll up to her face. "Guilty," she answered in a squeaky voice. She didn't move her lips.

"Then I sentence you to die," she said.

"Fair enough," the doll replied.

The girl does not seem to be a great actress, you may think. If a judge says, "You will die for your crimes," then you will say a lot of things. You may say, "Help!" or "Stone the crows." You would NOT say, "Fair enough."

"I hereby execute you!" she said suddenly and pulled off the doll's head.

"Ouch! That hurt!" the doll cried.

She pulled off the arms and then the legs. "Ouchy, ouchy-ouch!" the doll cried. "That'll teach everyone that you don't steal from a Sharkle, I suppose."

She threw the bits of doll on to the fire. Her father laughed. Her mother shook her head and tutted.

"Yes, that's the sort of thing we need to do in Wildpool. Make an example of the thieves," Silas Sharkle sighed. "But they won't let us tear off the heads of all the villains in Wildpool."

"Why not?" the girl asked.

"I don't know, my dear," the man said and spread his hands.

"We should leave everything to the police," Mrs Sharkle said.

"But what if the police are useless?" Charlotte asked.

"Our police are wonderful!" her mother cried.

Charlotte pulled a letter from the pouch that hung from her pink belt. She handed it to her father. "I just had this from Piggy Trotter at our school. See what she has to say."

Darlham Ladies College

2nd April 1837

Dearest Charlotte,

I hope you are well. The girls are so-o-o-o missing you. It was jolly rotten of Miss Peach to suspend you from school. I mean, all you did was put rat-poison in the teachers' salt cellar at dinner. The food is so rotten here the old dears didn't even taste the stuff. Miss Kilbey will be out of hospital soon so where's the harm? Miss Meldrum probably won't be back – ever. But she was old anyway. It's tennis season soon and they'll have to take you back. You're our star player, Lottie. I mean to say, it was April Fool's Day. What did they expect?

Anyway, our Papas pay their miserable teacher wages. (Except Bunty McGurgle, of course. They say her Pa has gone completely broke in some business deal. He can't afford to keep her here. Last we'll see of her, poor sop)

Silas Sharkle shook the letter. "Lottie, why am I reading this drivel?"

"Oh, Daddy, turn it over. See what Piggy says about Wildpool," the girl said.

The man turned over the paper and read.

On Saturday we went over to Wildpool to see our new yacht in the harbour. The coachman had left a rope trailing at the back of our carriage, careless clot. Anyway there were two policeman in the High Street. One stopped the carriage and said there was a rope hanging loose. Daddy said it was all right . . . it was our guard dog following behind. The fat policeman said there was nothing on the end of the rope. Daddy said it was an invisible dog. Then he took one of my marzipan sweets and asked the policeman to feed it to the dog! Would you believe it? The fat clown tried! He was crouched down saying, "Good boy, sweetie!" while the whole street watched. Then Daddy said, "April fool!" and we drove off. Oh, we laughed.

Anyway. Hope to see you back in school soon. Next week we start the school summer play and you definitely should have got the lead because you are the best actress ever.

Lots of love

Piggy

Silas Sharkle nodded slowly. "So, Lottie my dear . . . useless policemen . . . we need to do something, don't we?"

Chapter 3

MCGURGLE AND GUNS

Wednesday 5th April 1837

Gordon Griggsby, manager of the new bank, explained how money would be carried from the station to the bank on a cart with a locked strongbox. He left the students to work out how a gang of villains might rob it.

Nancy Turnip stood in front of the blackboard while Mr Dreep sat at the back of the classroom. "You are our expert at highway robbery, Nancy. Remind the class how we do it."

The girl blushed a little and pointed to a sketch of Wildpool High Street she had drawn. It showed the police station, the crime academy and

the new bank. On the sketch she had drawn an
"X" on the pavement and two Xs at the police
station.

"First you have to stop the coach," Nancy said.
"Any ideas how we'd do that?"

Smiff Smith raised a hand. "Please, miss, we could
throw Alice White in front of the horses! When they
trample her, the driver will have to stop. Great idea or
what?"

Nancy didn't laugh. Her serious face frowned.
"Yes. A great idea."

"Oh, thanks, Nance!" Alice cried.

"Yes," Millie Mixly said, excited. "But we don't
want Alice to get hurt."

"That's right," Martin agreed. "We just get Alice to
lie down in the middle of the road . . . pretend she's
been hit by a runaway horse. The driver will get down
to help her!"

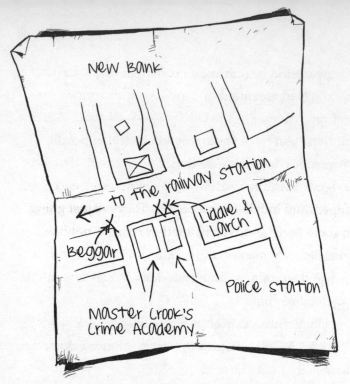

"Then two of us open the back of the cart and steal the loot?" Millie said.

"Hah!" Alice laughed a sharp and scornful laugh. "See that cross on the corner. That's the blind beggar that always sits there. He'll see what's happening and call the other two Xs . . . the constables at the front of the station. You'll be arrested before you get the doors open. Call yourselves crime academy students? You know nothing."

"The blind beggar won't see anything . . . he's blind!" Nancy argued.

"Yes . . . and I'm the Duchess of Wildpool," Alice snorted. "Anyway, the street will be full of people – farmers driving animals to the docks to sell, shoppers and street sellers, road-sweepers and sailors and singers and butchers and bakers. They are just going to stand there and watch, are they? This is not like your highwaymen on the heath, you know. This is a crowded street, you dummies. Master Crook would be ashamed of you."

Nancy's mouth fell open. Her lips moved. No words came out. The rest of the class looked at their desks.

"So what should they do, Alice?" Mr Dreep asked.

Alice marched to the front of the classroom and jabbed a thin finger at the map. "Millie stands on the corner here. She gives a signal when she sees the bank coach coming. I lie down in the road."

"Hope there's a farmer driving cattle to the docks!" Smiff chuckled.

"I – lie – down – at – the last – moment!" Alice said angrily. "The driver gets down. I tell him I want him

to carry me to the corner of Bridge Street. Then I say I need him to carry me all the way to the hospital on the north side of the bridge. The driver is right out of the way, see?"

"No," Smiff said. "How does that help?"

"Because *then* Nancy can climb up to the driving seat and take the whole cart away. We take it to a quiet spot. Smiff and Martin unload the loot. We open it in secret. No one sees us. Job done."

The class nodded. Mr Dreep's fingers rippled. "Gordon Griggsby said the police know about this test robbery. Even though we can use this to our advantage, this is to help them after all. Do you think they haven't thought of this?"

Alice rolled her eyes up to the ceiling. "They're cops. It's their cop brains against the brain of Alice White. Who do you think has the better brain?"

"A sheep has a better brain," Smiff said quietly.

"Or a beetle brain is better," Martin agreed.

"Even a Beadle brain," Smiff agreed. The boys' eyes twinkled as they waited for Alice to explode.

"OK class, now we have our plan. It's time for lunch." Mr Dreep led the class down to the kitchen

where he served up big bowls of hot tomato soup with bread and butter.

Tap! Tap! Tap!

There was a soft knock at the front door. Smiff went to answer it, as Nancy was helping to serve.

He opened the door to find a girl stood there. Her dress was plain, dark blue. Her face was just like a little china doll's. Her hair was dark and in ringlets and her hands were clutched nervously in front of her.

"Is this Master Crook's?" she asked in a voice as soft as tissue paper. "I desperately need your help."

Smiff couldn't help but smile at the girl and quickly ushered her through to the kitchen.

Mr Dreep jumped to his feet as Smiff brought in the nervous girl. "Come in, my dear. What's the matter?"

"Master Crook?" she asked.

"Master Crook is the owner of the school. I am one of his teachers," Samuel Dreep explained.

"May I join your school?" she asked shyly. Her voice was the voice of a lady and Alice's face twisted in disgust.

"Errrrgh! *May I join your school?*" she mimicked like a purple parrot.

Purple parrots are best. Forget your green-and-red parrots, your white cockatrices and your pink parakeets. You cannot beat a purple parrot. They taste really delicious with orange gravy and red onion sauce.

"Alice!" Samuel Dreep said sharply. "Remember the school rules!" He pointed to the list on the noticeboard. Alice didn't need to look to know what rule he meant. Rule ten.

BUT:

10 Pupils must **NOT** pick on other pupils. No matter how weedy and worthless a classmate looks they all have a place at Master Crook's. Be warned. Bully not or ye shall be bullied.

"Puh!" Alice said.

"Sit down," Mr Dreep said. "What's your name?"

"Bunty, sir. Bunty McGurgle."

"BUN-TEE!" Alice cried. "Mc-*GURGLE*! What sort of name is that?"

"It's *my* name," the girl breathed.

"Second and final warning, Alice," Mr Dreep said. The class had never seen him angry. He'd never had to punish anyone. Now it was like watching two people about to draw their guns in a western boy-cow gunfight.

"Mr Dreep, *sir*," Alice hissed. "Master Crook has a school for *poor* kids. Not for posh snobs like *Bunty McGurgle*."

"The school is for everyone who wants to see a world where money is shared around. A world where no one is poor."

Before Alice could reply Bunty put in, "We are poor, sir. My father was a rich man once, but then he fell in with a villain. That villain – his name was Silas Sharkle – took all our money and spent it on a trading ship. He filled it with muskets and cannons, powder and bullets. Then he sent it over the seas to the China seas where there was a war. He said we would sell the weapons to the war lords and get ten times our money back."

Samuel Dreep shook his head sadly. "Don't tell me. The ship sank?"

Bunty gasped. Even the class took a sharp breath. "How did you know?"

"An old, old trick," Samuel Dreep sighed. "He sent out an old, worm-eaten ship full of crates of scrap metal – not precious guns. The villain paid the crew to sail it out of sight and sink it. He kept the money that your father gave him."

"That's what I thought happened," Bunty whispered. "I came here hoping . . . hoping Master Crook could find a way to get our money back."

"What?" Alice jeered. "You want us to swim out and un-sink the ship?"

"No," Bunty said. "Mr Sharkle is putting all his money – *my Daddy's* money – in a new bank . . . Withering's Wildpool bank. I thought. . ."

"You *thought* we could get your rich Daddy's money *back* for him?" Alice shouted. "Well think again, brainless Bunty. We don't rob the rich to *pay* the rich, you posh-faced prawn. We're not here to risk the rope just so you can warm your white little hands and wear your blue little dresses and your bows and button-boots and crimp your curls with serving girls. . ."

"*Enough*, Alice," Mr Dreep said. "You were warned. There's the door . . . get out."

"What?" Alice blinked.

"You are suspended from the school for breaking rule ten. You can get back on the street corner where we found you – try selling matches for a day. It will give you time to cool off."

Alice snatched her shawl from the back of the chair and raced from the room. She slammed the door behind her as hard as she could.

In the silence of the kitchen it was lucky no one dropped a pin. It would have deafened the pupils.

At last Mr Dreep said, "Lunch is over, time to get back to lessons."

"What about the cart robbery, Mr Dreep?" Nancy asked.

"Bunty can take Alice's place there too. Can you lie down in the road and pretend to be hurt, Bunty?"

"Yes, sir," she said eagerly.

"Good! Then let's carry on with the plan, Nancy."

"Push off," Alice said.

The blind beggar, sitting on the corner of the High Street, looked up at her. "You what?"

"Are you deaf as well as blind?" the girl asked.

"No, but. . ."

"Then push off. I'm begging here for the next couple of days," the girl said.

"I *always* sit here!" the man argued. "I need the money to feed me poor little cat."

"It's a stuffed cat," Alice said. "What does it eat?"

"Stuffing," the man said.

"So get back to Wildpool workhouse and feed it. Or else."

"Or else what?"

"Or else I will report you to those two policemen," she said.

Liddle and Larch had just stepped out of the police station on their afternoon patrol and were sniffing the fresh April air. They could smell the fug from the gasworks and the fog from the coal-fires, the horse droppings, rats' nests and open toilet pits, the slime and grime from the shipyards on the riverside and the rotten stink of the river. But in the weak sun a few blades of grass were poking their brave heads through the cracks in the cobbles.

"Spring in the air," Larch said.

"Eh?" his thin-boned friend said.

"Spring in the air."

Liddle scratched his head. "Why should I?"

"Why should you what?"

"Why should I spring in the air? I mean, at my age, my bones aren't as young as they used to be. I might hurt myself, springing in the air like that. I'm not a rabbit you know."

"Officers!" Alice cried. "I wish to report a beggar."

"What do you want us to do about it?" Liddle asked.

"Arrest him."

"Oh, but we have to fill in so many forms!" Larch moaned. "Tell you what . . . we will get him to move along."

"Yes. Move along," Liddle said.

"Where to?" the beggar asked.

"Somewhere else. We've had a complaint. Move along."

The beggar picked up his cat and his cap full of money. "I was just off for a cup of tea anyway," he grumbled and stepped off the pavement. A greengrocer's cart full of carrots almost knocked him over. "Watch where you're going!" the greengrocer cried.

"Can't you see I'm blind?" the beggar shouted back.

"You need a guide dog then," the carrot cart driver called over his shoulder as he rattled off down the High Street.

"I've only got a guide cat."

"Not my problem," the carrot cart driver called as he vanished round a corner.

"Sometimes it's no fun being a blind beggar," the man moaned. But no one was listening. Constables Liddle and Larch were on the march. Alice and the beggar watched as they turned off the High Street and into a shop next door to the apothecary.

GEORGE GREEN
GUNSMITH

OPEN FOR ALL YOUR
PISTOLS, MUSKETS AND
HUNTING GUNS NEEDS

"Oh, dear," Alice whispered. "Oh, no! I wonder if Mr Dreep knows where they've gone? I have to warn him!" She ran towards Master Crook's Crime Academy. Then her boots skidded to a halt on the greasy cobbles. "No I *don't*," she said. "No I don't have to warn the miserable trout and little Miss McGurgle about anything. Let them find out the hard way. That'll teach them. Oh, yes. That'll *teach* them."

Liddle and Larch entered the shop. The shopkeeper, George Green, was small and bald and wore round glasses. "Good morning, gentlemen. I know what you've come for."

"The guns," Liddle said. "The special new guns you've made for us."

"They are ready. Come into the backyard and I will show you how they work."

Darkness fell over the grimy, gloomy streets of Wildpool. But in Master Crook's Crime Academy the gas lights gave off a cheering glow and the coal fires were warmer than toast.

The Mixlys and Smiff went home to their families.

In one of the bedrooms of the Academy Bunty McGurgle looked around and sniffed.

"That's your bed over there," Nancy said.

"There are no bedclothes on it!" Bunty gasped.

"No, the bedclothes are in the cupboard by the fireplace keeping warm," Nancy explained.

"But . . . but I can't make my *own* bed," Bunty gurgled. "At home I always had a servant to do it for me. *You* used to be a servant, Nancy, so *you* could do it for me, couldn't you, sweetie?"

"I suppose so," Nancy said and quietly took out the sheets and blankets. "I think Smiff likes you," she said with a shy smile.

"Lots of boys like me," Bunty sighed. "It's a nuisance. It's a curse, in fact. *Beauty* is *such* a *curse*. You should be pleased you have such a plain face, Nancy."

"Yes, miss."

"Oh! And I'd like a cup of tea in bed at nine o'clock tomorrow morning."

Nancy nodded.

"Two sugars."

Darkness fell over the grimy, gloomy streets of

Wildpool. And the last of the winter chill returned with it. Alice wrapped her shawl around her thin body and huddled in the doorway to the hat-seller's shop.

The hat-seller opened her door and looked down. "Here, a young girl like you shouldn't be trying to sleep there."

"No?" Alice said, hopeful. "You want to take me in and give me a cup of hot chocolate?"

"No, I want you to shove off and find another shop doorway to sleep in. You're making my place look untidy."

Alice moved down the road to the greengrocer shop and settled down again, this time with the smell of cabbage and carrot.

Constables Liddle and Larch wandered past. "Evenin' all!" they said. "Here, a young girl like you shouldn't be trying to sleep there."

"No? You want to take me to the station and give me some supper?"

"No. We want you in the workhouse. That's where homeless kids belong."

Alice let them lead her down Bridge Street and across to Wildpool's Wonderful Workhouse.

The old rosy-cheeked keeper, Miss Ruby Friday, opened the gate. "Oh, Alice! Lovely to see you!"

"I don't suppose you're going to give me hot chocolate or some supper?" she asked.

"No . . . I'm going to give you both! Come on in."

In the darkness the town hall clock chimed the end of the day. *Ding-dong, ding-dong, ding-dong. . .*

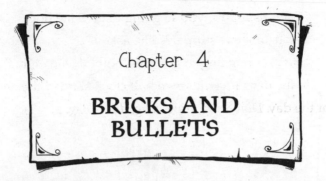

Chapter 4

BRICKS AND BULLETS

Friday 7th April 1837

Locomotive No. 3 pulled into Wildpool station with
a hiss of steam and a screech of cast-iron wheels on
cast-iron rails. The choking smoke from the chimney
floated up to the grimy glass roof of the station and
the soot drifted down like black snow.

Two horses munched their oats in nose-bags as
their wagon stood beside the railway carriage, waiting
to be loaded.

The wagon driver sat quietly reading the morning
newspaper. His dark eyebrows hung like curtains and
his beard was cut as square and heavy as a church door.

On the back of the four-wheeled cart was a box like

a large model of the bank. It was painted bright red with letters of gold.

Two railway porters heaved a heavy chest from the railway carriage. The chest was painted red and looked like an even smaller model of the bank – small enough to fit inside the bank on the back of the wagon.

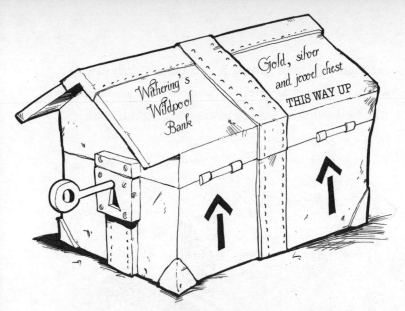

Martin Mixly stroked the ears of the horses, turned to his sister and said. "It's as if they *want* someone to steal it."

"They *do* . . . this time. Us! But it's full of bricks, isn't it?" she said.

Martin nodded. "That's what Gordon Griggsby told us." He looked towards the groups of people who stood around the station buildings.

There were ragged men and women in shivering huddles in the shadows. There were rich men with gold watches on chains, tucked into fine silk waistcoats, and with thick whiskers bristling under

finer silk top hats. The women with the rich men carried parasols as bright as parrots and wore bonnets trimmed with the best lace. They warmed their white hands in fur gloves.

Yes, the ladies warmed their hands in dead animals. They wore dead animals around their necks and trimmed their dresses with dead animals. They still do! Some women wear so much fur they are scared to go into the forest in case a hunter shoots them. Why do they do it? I ask. What's it all fur?

"*We* know it's full of bricks," Martin nodded, "but those thieves don't. They may try to rob it before we do!"

"No," the driver of the carriage said suddenly. His white teeth glinted through the dark beard. "They will watch and see what happens. They will not try to rob it this time."

"But if they see *us* get away with it they will try next time," Martin argued.

"Hah!" the driver laughed. "But you won't get away with it. They will see you caught and they will never try to rob a Withering's bank wagon ever again."

Millie scowled at him. "We have a great plan," she said.

"So do the police," the driver said with a shrug. He jumped down and slipped the nose-bags off the horses. The cart springs groaned as the heavy chest was slid inside the back door of the van. The porters groaned and wiped sweat from their brows.

"It's done, driver!" one of them called. The driver tipped his hat in thanks. (The porters wanted him to tip them with some money. No chance. The driver's wallet was closed as tight as an oyster.)

That is how he became so rich.

"Buy my matches!" Alice cried in a pitiful voice. "Buy a poor girl's matches."

The sign by her side was scrawled on the back of an old advert for shoe polish.

MATCHES

BUY THESE MATCHES FROM THE POOR
LITTLE MATCH GIRL WHO IS TRYING TO
FEED HER MOTHER, FATHER AND TEN
BROTHERS AND SISTERS.
1P A BOX.
SPECIAL OFFER
BUY ONE GET 2 FOR 2P

"I'll buy a box of your matches," the blind beggar said.

"I haven't got any."

"Not got any matches?"

"No."

"So you can't sell me any?"

"That's right," Alice nodded.

"So . . . so, why are you shouting, 'Buy my matches'? Eh?" the beggar asked.

Alice gave a long sigh. "I am a spy. I am here to see what's going on in the street. The match selling is just a cover story. No one will think I'm spying. They'll think I am selling matches."

The blind beggar nodded. He watched the spring lambs being driven towards the quayside and the shoppers with their baskets prodding potatoes, squeezing sausages and sniffing scented soaps.

"Wouldn't it be a good idea to have a few matches to sell?" the beggar said after a while.

"Nah! I might get arrested by the police for begging," she explained.

"Right," the blind beggar nodded. He stroked his stuffed cat and leaned against the wall of the hat shop.

"So what are you spying on?"

Alice looked towards the corner of the street where Smiff Smith stood. A red wagon was trundling along from the station. Smiff waved a hand to someone across the road from Alice . . . a girl in a blue dress. "I'm spying on a robbery," Alice said.

The slow wagon was being followed by fifty eyes as the gangs of thieves from the station followed it. "Those ragged people going to rob it?" the beggar asked.

"No-o-o! They're hopeless thieves! That's why they're ragged! It's the ones in fine clothes that will try."

"They look rich!"

"Of course they do!" Alice groaned. "That's what I'm saying! They are *rich* because they are *good* robbers. They're the ones the bank will have to watch. You are as brainless as your cat."

Oh dear. What a cruel thing to say! I hope you're never that cruel. And it wasn't even a clever thing for Alice to say! The blind beggar's cat had a big brain. Yes, it was a brain made of cotton wool, but that's not the point. What is the point? I don't know.

57

"Suppose so," the blind beggar nodded.

"Now, let's see what a mess Master Crook's clowns can make of the robbery," she smirked.

The girl in the blue dress waved back at Smiff and stepped off the pavement. She pushed her way through a flock of lazy lambs, threw the back of her hand to her forehead and gave a cry. "Woe!"

"Whoa!" Alice gasped. "Whoa? Is she trying to stop a horse?"

"Woe is me!" Bunty McGurgle cried even louder and staggered into the road. The shoppers and the gangs of thieves stopped to watch. Shopkeepers came to their doors and even the lambs gazed as hard as they usually grazed.

"I think I am going to faint!" Bunty croaked.

"I think I am going to be sick," Alice spat. "That is the worst acting I have seen since the dancing cow in the Christmas show at the Apollo Music Hall."

"I thought it was a good dancing cow," the beggar said.

"It fell off the stage into the orchestra!" Alice cried. "It climbed out with a French horn stuck on its head."

"All cows have horns on their heads," the beggar said.

"Shut up," Alice said.

Bunty fell slowly, and carefully, into the road – she found a patch where there were no sheep or horse droppings and lay down.

The wagon driver said, "Whoa!"

"*He's* at it now," Alice muttered. The driver climbed down and raised Bunty's head.

"Thank you, sir," she whispered.

"Poor child," Silas Sharkle said. "Can I help?"

You should have already guessed Silas Sharkle was driving the wagon. You had enough clues. They were staring you in the face and if you didn't see them then you should get a job as a blind beggar.

"You can carry me home, sir," she said. "Take me to the Wonderful Wildpool Workhouse across the river."

"Climb on to the wagon and I'll drive you there!" he offered.

"No!" the girl squawked . . . then remembered she was supposed to be faint. "No . . . I suffer wagon-sickness. Carry me there, good sir . . . Miss Friday, the kindly workhouse keeper will care for me!"

Silas Sharkle picked Bunty McGurgle up and

marched to the corner of High Street where he turned into Bridge Street. As soon as he was out of sight Smiff Smith darted out from a shop doorway and jumped up on to the driving seat. He released the brake and cracked the whip.

The carriage rolled forward and the horses seemed to sense he was in a hurry. They broke into a canter and clattered through leaping lambs.

YOU would leap if a pair of charging horses were heading towards you.

The cobbles clattered as the wheels whirred and the steel rims struck sparks. The gangs of thieves were too surprised to move but Alice knew what to expect and she was scurrying towards the east end of the High Street. She was just in time to see the wagon skid round into the back lane behind Low Street.

Women had hung out their washing in the spring breeze and it flapped in Smiff's face. He tore bloomers from his brows, trousers from his teeth, and knickers from his nostrils. He tugged on the reins as he reached a back gate where a woman waited. Her hair was like a bird's nest – only not so tidy and not so clean.

"Hello, Ma," Smiff grinned. "Is Nancy there?"

Smiff's schoolmate was in the yard with a rope ready to drag the treasure chest out. "Open the door, Smiff, we'll hide the chest under a heap of coal here. Then you can drive on to the docks and dump the wagon."

Smiff walked to the back of the wagon. "We'll break up the chest for firewood and even if they search the whole of Wildpool they'll never find out where their treasure went."

Nancy sighed. "Shame it's only a box full of bricks. The plan is perfect!"

Smiff shrugged and threw open the back door of the wagon. Inside was gloomy. Not a lot of sunlight fell between the high walls of the black-bricked back lane. Even less fell inside a covered wagon in that lane.

The chest sat there, glowing a dull red.

And behind it were two white circles. Smiff squinted hard. The circles were two pale faces. Beneath them four pale hands held silver tubes.

The faces smiled. "Mornin' all!" Constable Liddle said.

"Put your hands up or we will shoot," Constable

Larch added.

"Run, Nancy, run!" Smiff cried.

Mrs Smith darted back into her yard and bolted the door. Smiff grabbed Nancy by the arm and tugged her up the lane towards the safety of Master Crook's Crime Academy.

"Stop or we will shoot," Constable Larch called after them. The constables stood in the doorway and raised their rifles.

"They'll shoot us!" Nancy cried as she struggled.

"No they won't!" Smiff argued. "They're too soft. They wouldn't harm a fly."

Constables Liddle and Larch fired their weapons. *Crack! Crack!*

Which just goes to show. . .

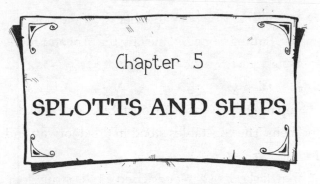

Chapter 5

SPLOTTS AND SHIPS

Saturday 8th April 1837

. . . something.

The newspaper told the amazing tale.

THE WILDPOOL STAR

8 April 1837

BANK ROBBERS 'BUNGLED'

Wildpool's wonderful policemen, Constables Liddle and Larch showed the world just how hard it's going to be to rob Withering's bank. With the help of some fake thieves, the bank set up a fake robbery to test the security of the bank and the skill of Wildpool's police force.

Little did the fake thieves know that the cunning constables were concealed under the cover at the back of the wagon.

Constable Liddle told our reporter, "Little did they know we were concealed under the cover at the back of the wagon."

Constable Larch joked, "You could say, Liddle did they know! Hah! Hah!"

The driver of the wagon was the rich businessman Silas Sharkle. "Stopping the thieves is easy – you just need an armed guard. But catching them alive is the tricky part.

And that's where my amazing invention is so brilliant," he said. "The net gun can catch them alive so we can hang them in front of Darlham Gaol. That will show every villain for fifty miles you can't steal from a Sharkle."

Mr Sharkle's invention was made by Wildpool gunsmith, George Green. He told our reporter, "The net gun doesn't fire bullets – it fires a short dart like a harpoon. Fastened to the end of the dart is a rope and a net. The officers aim over the head of the fleeing thieves. The nets drops on them and they are caught."

Mayor Oswald Twistle said he planned to give the courageous constables another medal to add to their collection. "There will be no crime in Wildpool as long as I am mayor!" he said. "Vote for me next month."

Wildpool Star has a sketch of the wonderful new crime-cracking weapon, free to all readers. Collect it from the offices and pay just two shillings for delivery.

Little match girl Alice White said, "I saw it all. What a bunch of bungling buffoons. They couldn't steal milk from a cat. Heh! Heh! Serves them right." Our reporter was unable to find out just what served the thieves right.

The pupils of Master Crook's Crime Academy looked at the sketch that Samuel Dreep stuck to the blackboard. It had come free with the newspaper.

"It's clever," he said and tugged at his side-whiskers.

"It's cheating," Smiff snarled. "How's an honest

bank-robber supposed to make a living when they come up with weapons like that?"

Nancy studied the plan. She shook her head. "No. I can't see any way round it. They have us beat."

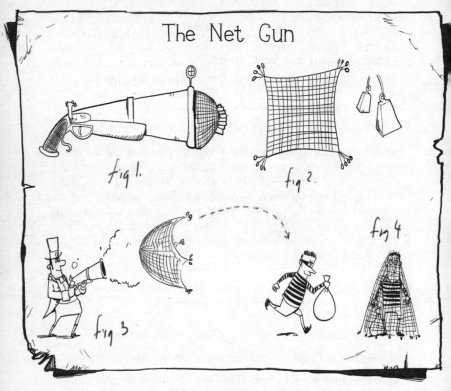

The Net Gun

fig 1.

fig 2.

fig 3.

fig 4.

When the train pulled out of Wildpool station that day it was filled with thieves. The ragged failed thieves

and the rich successful thieves left the town. They left behind crumpled copies of the newspaper. They left behind broken dreams.

They went off to simpler crimes like stealing sheep from sheds or whipping washing from lines, pinching pennies from poor-boxes in church or snaffling sausages from butchers' stalls.

"No one can rob Withering's Wildpool bank," a man in a golden waistcoat moaned.

"You could walk in with a gun and threaten to shoot the manager, Gordon Griggsby," the woman in the emerald dress told him.

The man gave her a sour look. "I am an honest thief . . . not some American boy-cow," he said.

Monday 10th April 1837

But in Master Crook's Crime Academy the students did not give in so easily.

Dreep faced his students. "Now, class, we used this test as an opportunity to discover the bank's strengths and weaknesses. Is there any way to escape the net gun?"

"We could carry a pair of sheep shears," Smiff said, "and snip our way out of the net!"

Millie Mixly nodded. "Yes . . . you could *get away* doing that . . . but you still wouldn't have the chest of treasure, would you?"

"It looks like there's no way round it. The treasure is safe in the bank wagon," Nancy said.

Martin Mixly sighed, "I wish Alice was here. She'd think of a way. She has the brain of a great criminal."

"Yes, and the great criminal wants it back," Smiff snorted. "We can do this without awful Alice," he said.

Bunty McGurgle raised the back of her hand to her brow. "Poor little Alice. Where is the dear little child? Still on the street selling matches? Oh, what a waste of a sweet young life! I feel it was all my fault."

"She was rotten to you," Nancy said.

"I forgive her," Bunty said and fluttered her eyelashes like an angel.

As you know angels flutter their eyelashes a lot. It helps them to fly. Those wings are not enough. They also grow their toenails long and flutter them too. At least that's what I was told by the last angel I met.

"You're very kind," Nancy said.

"Thank you," Bunty said and brushed away a tear.

"You're the nicest person I know," Smiff sighed. "Twice as clever as Alice and ten times as pretty."

"Thank you," Bunty said and pushed a handkerchief to her lips to choke back a sob.

Martin Mixly looked at his sister and put two fingers down his throat as if to throw up. Millie nodded. "Smiff's brain is turning to water," she murmured.

"Alice can return when she says sorry," Mr Dreep said. "Now, let's get back to the problem we have to solve. The bank is almost finished. It will be filled with gold and silver, jewels and priceless works of art before the week is out. Master Crook needs us to set the treasure free so we can care for the poor and needy in Wildpool."

"Please, sir," Bunty said. "If Master Crook is such a *master*, then why can't *he* come up with a plan?"

"How would you learn if Master Crook always gave you the answer?" Samuel Dreep asked. "But he does like to help along the way so at ten o'clock we will have a guest who can help us with our problem." Dreep pulled a cheap watch from his waistcoat pocket and looked at it. The clock on the town hall chimed the hour. *Ding-dong, ding-dong, ding-dong. . .*

There was a knock at the door. Nancy trotted off to

answer it. She led a man into the classroom. He wore a brown corduroy suit that was stretched over a body that seemed to be made of granite. His weathered face was as rough as a rock too and his cap sat on his thick hair like a saucer on a lion's mane.

"Welcome, Mr Craggs!" Samuel Dreep cried and reached out a thin, twiggy-fingered hand to their guest.

Craggs shook hands with the teacher. There was a crackling of bones and a whimper of pain from Samuel Dreep. "Ooooh!" He pulled his hand free and shook away the pain. "Welcome to Master Crook's Crime Academy . . . Class, this is Mr Norman Craggs from Wildpool shipyard."

Craggs looked at the class a little shyly. "I've never taught in a school before," he said. "In fact I've never been inside a school."

"No, but you are a master of the new art of building iron ships, Mr Craggs," Samuel Dreep said.

"It's my job," the man said with a shrug.

"So . . . we're going to get an iron ship, sail it up the High Street straight into Withering's Wildpool bank are we?" Smiff jeered.

The teacher ignored him and turned to the ship builder.

70

"You are so good at building watertight, iron ships the bank has given you a special task, haven't they?"

"They have. They asked me to build their thief-proof safe," Craggs said.

"Now my class are very interested in safes . . . and crime . . . and Master Crook invited you here to show the students how you build a thief-proof safe. What are its strengths . . ."

"And its weaknesses," Smiff said.

Norman Craggs pulled a piece of paper from his pocket and unfolded it. The teacher copied it on to the blackboard.

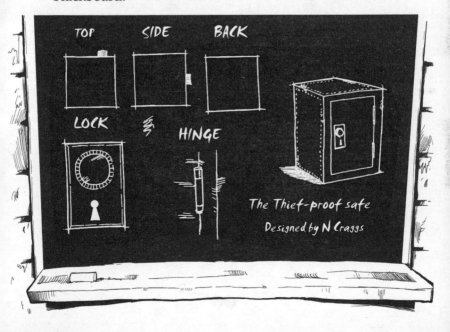

And for half an hour the class tried to find a way into the safe. There were two locks. One key was held by Gordon Griggs, the bank manager. The other key would be held by his chief clerk.

"We could kidnap the manager and the clerk. . ." Smiff began.

"What do you mean?" Norman Craggs said, alarmed.

Samuel Dreep stepped forward and said quickly, "It's a game! We sometimes *pretend* to be criminals so we can see how their minds work. What Smiff *meant* to say was a *criminal gang* could kidnap the key-holders and force them to open the safe."

Craggs nodded. "That's why Mayor Twistle has said the manager and the clerk must be armed with a pistol at all times. If anyone tries to take the key they will be shot."

"Oh! Oh! Oh!" Bunty McGurgle cried. "I am fainting at the very thought. Shot on the spot with my blood going splott."

"Don't worry, Bunty," Smiff said softly. "I would stand between you and the gun if I had to."

Bunty's mouth turned down. "Thank you Smiff,

72

dear, but then it would be *your* blood that went splott on my clean blue dress. It's bad enough to have one's own blood, but to have someone else's blood is just too, too hideous! If you have to bleed please do it well away from me!"

"Sorry, Bunty," Smiff said.

Mr Dreep spread his hands. "Thank you *so* much, Mr Craggs. The class are happy knowing the thief-proof safe will keep the riches of Wildpool safe."

Craggs smiled and stretched out a hand to say goodbye. Mr Dreep said, "Nancy, please show our guest to the door."

"It's impossible," Bunty McGurgle said.

"Ah, but Master Crook's Crime Academy students enjoy the impossible, don't we?" the teacher asked.

Millie and Martin nodded excitedly. Smiff just looked at Bunty while saliva dribbled down his chin.

"What can we do now, Mr Dreep?" Millie asked.

"Go to the theatre, Millie," the teacher said. "Tonight we will all go to the theatre."

"Buy my matches!" Alice sang on the street corner. She sat under the canopy of the hat-seller's shop window.

"Buy a poor girl's matches."

MATCHES FOR SALE
BUY MY MATCHES OR SEE ME STARVE.
DO YOU WANT THAT?
NO? THEN PUT MONEY IN MY MATCH TRAY.
LOVE FROM ALICE
P.S. JUST DON'T ASK FOR ANY MATCHES.

"Mornin' all!" Constables Liddle and Larch said. They wore Mayor Oswald Twistle's shiny brass medals with pride.

"Morning, constables," Alice said.

"You're not *begging,* are you?" Constable Liddle asked and his thin moustache dripped a little from the April shower that had just blown over.

"Begging?" Alice cried. "How *dare* you."

"Sorry, but I only asked because—"

"Yes, yes," she said, jumping to her feet. "Now shut up and get out of my way. I want to see what's going on over the road."

The policemen stepped back and followed Alice's stare. Wagons were rolling up from the riverside and

the sweating horses stopped outside the bank. Each cart held a part of the safe. Alice counted the three walls, a side with a cut-out for the door, the square roof to the safe and the heavy door itself.

"It's the thief-proof safe," Constable Larch said.

Alice smiled. "Thief-proof? Who says? You says? I think not. Oh, no. Not thief-proof at all. But I wonder if those dummies in Master Crook's Crime Academy have worked out how to rob it?"

And I wonder if you have? Maybe you don't have the mighty criminal brain of Alice White. In that case you will have to read on to find out how to crack Withering's thief-proof safe.

Chapter 6

MAGIC AND MONKEYS

Monday 10th April 1837

In the evening the Apollo Music Hall glittered under the gas lamps and looked like a magical palace.

In the grey daylight it looked like a shop that sells shoddy and was as shabby as a sixty-year-old slipper. But in the evening it shone – warm and welcoming.

The board outside promised the most marvellous and mellifluous melange of mind-boggling masterpieces ever to be seen on a star-spangled stage for superior supporters of sparklingly supreme sophistication and evenings of endless elegant and erudite entertainment.

The poster that week would tempt any tightwads to cough up their coins.

APOLLO MUSIC HALL, WILDPOOL

SOLE LESSEE MR FARLAND PROUDLY PRESENTS

A GRAND VOCAL INSTRUMENTAL THESPIAN AND TERPSICHOREAN FESTIVAL

THE WEEK OF 10TH APRIL 1837 AT 8.00 P.M.

COMIC DUETTISTS
FOR THIS WEEK ONLY,
MISS JULIA & MISS NELLIE VEZIN. MUSIC AND LAUGHTER FROM THE TWO LOVELY LADIES

DRAMA
"Your Life's In Danger", a farce in which Mr Jordan will sing the local song, *"Does your Mother know you are out?"*

IRISH COMEDIAN
Mr Jerry Farrisey. Eminent entertainer from the Emerald Isle

VENTRILOQUIST
Mr F Renhard. The only lips that move are the lips of his puppet, Lord Wibble

MAGIC
The Fakir of Ava will do tricks that are the eighth wonders of the world. Seeing is believing!

SENSATION
Old Mother Hubbard and her wonderful dog!
Clever canine capers

SENTIMENTAL SINGER
Mr F W Montague. If you have tears prepare to shed them

MELODRAMA
"The Alarming Sacrifice" starring Matilda Heron, with her stock company from the "Adelphi Theatre" in London

DANCE
"La Zingarella," with Mr Smith and Miss Annie Walters

PRESIDER : MR EDWIN VILLIERS.
STAGE MANAGER : MR A MAYNARD
CHAIRMAN : MR T NORRIS
ORCHESTRA LEADER : MR WILSON
PIANIST : MR SOLOMON

Admission: Boxes 1 shilling; Balcony 9 pence; Stalls 6 pence; Back seats 4 pence.
Entertainment will start at 8:00p.m. doors will open half an hour earlier.
No dogs, no drinking your own drink, no spitting and ladies are not allowed
to smoke. Food and drink are served at the intervals, before and after the show.

A REWARD OF 20 SHILLINGS WILL BE PAID BY
THE MANAGEMENT ON THE DETECTION
AND CONVICTION OF PERSONS DESTROYING
OR MUTILATING THE POSTERS OF THIS THEATRE.

The pupils from Master Crook's Crime Academy walked through the stage door behind Mr Dreep. "Where are we going?" Smiff demanded. "I want to see the show."

"And so you shall, Smiff. But first I want you to meet a friend of mine."

"Is he in the show?" Millie Mixly asked, excited. "Is he famous? I always wanted to meet someone famous."

"Ooooh!" Bunty McGurgle cooed. "If I met someone famous I'd faint."

"Don't worry, I'd catch you before you fell to the floor," Smiff promised.

This time Millie joined her brother in sticking fingers down her throat. Nancy caught sight of them and smiled.

Mr Dreep tapped on a dressing-room door.

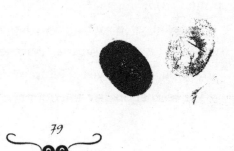

FAKIR OF AVA
CHIEF OF STAFF OF CONJURORS, TO
HIS SUBLIME GREATNESS
THE NANKA OF ARISTAPHAE

"What's a *fakir*?" Smiff asked. "Someone that goes around *faking* things?"

"A *fakir* is an Eastern Holy Man who has magical powers . . . Ava is in Burma," Samuel Dreep explained.

"Come in!" a voice called from inside the room.

The teacher opened the door and the students of

orchestra, just in front of the stage, played a jolly tune and the burbling audience settled down. They didn't just come to watch – they came to join in.

The class's favourite was Irish comedian, Mr Jerry Farrisey. He started his comic song and a sheet rolled down from above the stage so they could all join in with his song about a trip to Wildpool beach.

Martha swallowed a jellyfish,
Janie got the cramp,
My ma-in-law began to roar
because the sea was damp!
While I was floundering through the waves,
A crab got 'old of me!
And when we looked for the bathing-machine,
It had drifted out to sea.

The evening romped along like a playful pony – except there weren't any ponies in the show. Just dancing dogs and a monkey that walked a tightrope.

Then the crowd's cheers died down to silence.

A back-cloth dropped down to fill the stage. It was painted with a scene from an eastern market. There were stalls painted with weird fruits, mud-walled houses and a domed temple.

Then the stage manager covered the spotlight with blue glass and the whole scene looked like a moonlit night. The orchestra played eastern music.

The chairman, Mr Norris, spoke in a hushed, hoarse voice from his platform at the side of the stage. "At this point in the entertainment we ask that nervous ladies leave the theatre – you will see the dreadful death of a simple serving lad, live on this very stage and before your very eyes. See his head severed with a slice from the sharpest scimitar this side of Suez."

"Ooooh!" the audience cooed. No one left. Not even the nervous ladies.

"If you stay you will see the weirdest, most wondrous events ever seen in Wildpool's Apollo theatre. Put your hands together in awe and amazement for Burma's most brilliant beheading beast . . . the Fakir of Ava, Chief of Staff of Conjurors to His Sublime Greatness the Nanka of Aristaphae."

"*Ooooh!*"

"I give you . . . the Fakir of Ava!"

Applause shook the walls of the hall and feet stamped on the floors, raising clouds of sawdust in the smoky air.

Sawdust? you cry! Yes, I know you go to the theatre today, in 1901, and expect to see carpets. Sawdust is for the filthy taverns that fester in awful alleys. Sawdust soaks up the spit and spilled ale. Yes, dear reader, the sawdust in the Apollo was there for just the same reason . . . in 1837 the spitters and spillers spat and spilled in the theatres.

Isaiah Hughes glided on to the stage and began his magic act. The dim blue light helped to hide his hands as he produced a boy from a bowl of water. Then the boy's head was sliced off as ladies screamed in terror.

Isaiah the Fakir held up the head so the blue eyes gleamed in the blue spotlight. Then he covered it with a hood and placed it back on the boy's shoulders. He covered it all with a cloth and when the cloth was removed the boy jumped up, screamed when he saw the sword and ran off the stage.

Now the audience laughed.

Martin said, "It's not so much fun when you know

how he did it," and the others agreed.

But they fell silent as the Fakir of Ava spoke for the first time. "Iggle, glumpa wompo lickety duck!"

The chairman said, "Ladies and gentlemen, the Fakir has asked for a young lady to help with his next trick. . ."

"Nuppa-luppa, choppa uppa!"

"But he says the lady will NOT have her head chopped off!"

A woman in the front row called out, "Here! I'll have a go," and she was cheered as the chairman helped her up the steps to the stage. "What is your name, young lady?"

"Peggy Maginty," the girl said.

Fakir Isaiah led her to one of the striped market stalls that was more like a sentry box for a soldier on guard. He waved a hand to show he wanted young Peggy to look around it. She walked around and rapped on it.

"Solid as my boyfriend's head!" she said.

The Fakir opened the door and waved her inside. She trembled and giggled as she stepped into the box. The magician closed the door and rapped on the box. Peggy Maginty knocked back.

The drummer in the orchestra gave a long rattle on the drum as the Fakir waved his hands and cried, "Abracadabra!"

He threw open the door to the box . . . and Peggy's face looked out, "Coo-ee!"

The audience groaned.

The Fakir looked annoyed and tried again. He closed the window then picked up a chain. He wrapped it around the box twice and fastened it with a padlock so no one could get out.

Then he threw a large sheet over the box.

This time he shouted "Abracadabra-cadabra-cadabra!"

He took his slicing scimitar sword and pushed it through a joint in the box. The tip of the sword came through the other side. The audience gasped.

"*Ooooh!*"

Let's face it, YOU would gasp if you saw a sword being stuck through a young lady. Of course you would gasp a lot MORE if the sword was stuck through you. There is nothing so gasp-making as a blood-soaked sword sticking through your chest. It makes me gasp just to think of it. Gasp!

"Here!" the chairman wailed. "You said the lady would not be hurt!"

The Fakir seemed to go into a rage. He picked up three more swords and jabbed them into the box. Even the gentlemen in the audience were screaming now.

Isaiah the Fakir raised his arms high above his head and the audience fell silent. Then he unwrapped the chain, took hold of the door and peered inside. He turned to the audience and gave a blue-toothed smile. He flung the door wide. Four swords criss-crossed the inside of the box.

But Peggy Maginty was gone.

The chairman strode down from his platform on to the stage. He pulled out the swords, stepped into the box and rattled all the sides. "Amazing! I thought there must be a hidden compartment . . . but there isn't. Would any gentleman from the audience care to examine the box?" Several men came forward, rattled the box, rapped it, tapped it, tipped it, poked, prodded and picked at it. They left, shaking their heads.

The chairman spread his hands in wonder. "Peggy Maginty has vanished into thin air!"

Smiff leaned across to Bunty. "The chairman is part of the act."

"Really?" the girl breathed.

"Oh, yes. And so is that Peggy Maginty."

"Oh, Smiff, you are so very clever," Bunty squealed.

"I know," Smiff said.

"So?"

"So what?"

"So how did he do the trick? I mean, where did she really go?"

"Ah . . . ummm . . . ahhhh. . ." Smiff stammered.

"We'll go back stage after the show and ask him, shall we?" Samuel Dreep said.

"What has this to do with robbing a bank?" Nancy asked him.

"Maybe nothing . . . maybe everything. If Isaiah knows how to make a girl disappear from inside a locked box then maybe he can help us make money disappear from inside a locked safe."

The act ended with the chairman opening the door to the box. Peggy staggered out and cried, "Ooooh! I had the strangest dream – I dreamed I was in Burma."

"Uppa-cuppa boogle woo!" the Fakir said.

The chairman explained, "The Fakir says that's because you WERE in a village in Burma – the Fakir magicked you there!"

"Ooooh!" Peggy sighed. "Fancy *that*!"

The audience cheered, long and loud, the Fakir took his bow and the show carried on.

At the back of the theatre, Alice White stood and watched with a faint smile. "Very clever, Master Crook – you've given your class all they need to rob Withering's Wildpool bank. There's only one thing going to stop you pulling it off. One little thing. . ." she said.

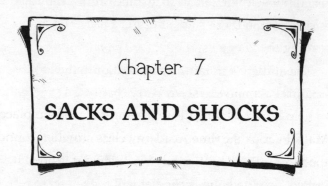

Chapter 7

SACKS AND SHOCKS

Isaiah Hughes was scrubbing off the face-colour when the class crowded into the dressing room after the show.

"Splendid show, Isaiah," Samuel Dreep said.

"Not bad," the Fakir of Ava chuckled. "So, did you spot how I did the disappearing girl?"

"That Peggy was part of the act," Smiff said. "And so was the chairman."

"And the gentlemen from the audience?"

"No-o-o," Smiff admitted. "They gave it a good looking-at and they didn't see a back door. Peggy didn't slip out the back."

The magician soaped his face and washed it then dried himself with a towel. "Come on stage and have a look yourself," he said, slipping a jacket on and leading the way.

The theatre was empty now but the smell of the audience remained. Isaiah Hughes asked a stagehand to help him move the disappearing cabinet into place. Master Crook's Crime Academy class crowded round the box and rattled it, rapped it, tapped it, tipped it, poked, prodded and picked at it.

Bunty McGurgle cried, "I know how he did it!"

The class turned to her in surprise.

"How?"

"It was magic! He magicked her away to Burma," Bunty whispered.

The Fakir shook his head. "If I was that clever I'd magic myself into your bank, load up with money and magic myself back out. I wouldn't be sweating on stinking stages like Wildpool Apollo for five shillings a night! No, I cheated." He stepped inside the box but left the door open. He waved to the stagehand at the side of the stage. The man turned a handle.

93

The class groaned as they saw the floor of the box open and allow Isaiah to lower himself through a trapdoor in the stage. He waved goodbye.

The stagehand turned the handle the other way and the trapdoor and the floor of the box closed again. Isaiah had stepped off beneath the stage. The box was empty.

A minute later the Fakir appeared from the side of the stage. "There's a lot of room under that stage. Peggy can go out the side door, the way I just did, and disappear forever! Or she can step back on the lift and pop back into the box."

"So, it's not magic after all?" Bunty said, a little disappointed.

"Not real magic," Isaiah said.

"But it helps us rob that bank. Doesn't it?"

"It does," Nancy said.

"It does," Millie and Martin Mixly said.

"Does it?" Bunty McGurgle asked.

"Remember the plan of the safe that Norman Craggs showed us?" Smiff asked. "It had three walls, a door and a roof – all too solid to cut through."

"But it doesn't have a metal floor!" Nancy said.

"We get into the bank and dig under the safe . . . we come up inside. Perfect!"

Tuesday 11th April 1837

Millie Mixly was given the job of writing the shopping list.

Bank robbery shopping list

4 mining shovels

4 miners' pick-axes

4 saws

5 sacks marked "Loot"

5 dark lanterns

5 pairs of gloves (small)

Smiff and Nancy were given the money to go to the ironmongers at the end of Low Street.

Outside hung tin pots and clothes-pegs, china cups and pewter mugs. They stepped inside and made their way through the piles of ropes and riddle, candles and cart-grease, buckets and brooms, knives and forks, hammers and handsaws.

The thin old owner, as grey as February, peered at the boy. "You again," he said. "You're not after cheating me out of another mop bucket, are you? You're out of luck cos I'm out of mop buckets. Some woman keeps coming in and buying them."

"That'll be my Ma," Smiff sighed. "She reckons you can never have too many mop buckets."

"Woman with hair like a bird's nest? Seems she's come into a bit of money," the old man said.

"I make a good living now," Smiff nodded.

"So what can I do for you?"

Smiff passed the list across the counter. The old man disappeared into the back of the shop and came back with the items on the list. "Now, son. I haven't any bags with 'Loot' on them but I have these," he said. He showed Smiff the bags.

Bag used in the Great Wildpool Bank Robbery, 1837
Property of Wildpool Museum

"They'll have to do," Smiff said.

You can see the bag in Wildpool Museum. But which careless criminal from Master Crook's class left this clue behind? Or were they all caught? Wait and see.

"Sorry we don't have 'loot'. The 'loot' bags are very popular with the criminals in the county. You see, if the police stop them, and ask them what they're carrying, they say they have *tools* in the bag. When the police ask why it has 'loot' written on, the villains say they spelled 'tools' backwards so no one would pinch their tools. See?"

"Not really," Smiff sighed. "How much do we owe you?"

"Two guineas . . . but since you're such a good customer I'll let you have the lot for two pounds."

Smiff nodded and handed the money over. He and Nancy loaded everything into a wheelbarrow at the front door to the shop and trundled it back along to Master Crook's Crime Academy.

"He charged us too much," Nancy said.

"I know," Smiff laughed.

"So what's so funny?" she asked.

"The old thief was so pleased with himself, he didn't notice we went off with one of his wheelbarrows! Heh! Heh!"

Wednesday 12th April 1837

The class were shocked, stunned, dazed, flabbergasted – their flabbers had never been so gasted – dumbfounded more than their founds had ever been dumbed. They were astonished.

A man stood in front of the class who looked like Samuel Dreep with his red-and-white scarf and shabby top hat. He even had Mr Dreep's gooseberry-green eyes and those fingers that were as fine as twigs on a vine, and that rippled when he talked.

But the face was brown as the Fakir of Ava, the side-whiskers were shaved and the hair as short as a worn yard-brush.

"Good morning, class," the figure said – and he even had Mr Dreep's voice.

No one answered. The man grinned. "So? Do you like my disguise?"

"Mr Dreep?" Nancy asked. "It's wonderful – except you've spread a bit of brown boot polish on your collar. It gives you away a bit."

"It's a fine day today. I want you to go into the back garden of the academy and practise your digging. You can even plant a few vegetables while you are there. The seeds are in the kitchen dresser."

"Where will you be, Mr Dreep – while we do all the hard work?"

"Finding you an easy way to get inside the bank," the man said and tapped his nose. He left a white spot where the polish rubbed off.

The class gathered the pick-axes and spades and went into the garden. "Ohhhh!" Bunty McGurgle sighed. "My poor hands are too soft and feeble to hold a spade. Nancy can do my share of the digging, can't

you Nancy?"

"Yes, Bunty."

"I'll do some too," Smiff offered.

"Good idea!" the girl in the blue dress cried. "Smiff can start while Nancy makes me a cup of tea."

"Yes, Bunty."

"Two sugars."

Gordon Griggsby stood in front of the new bank building and looked at it proudly. The last tiles were being placed on the roof. A brass sign was being screwed on to the deep-red front doors. . .

Withering's Wildpool Bank

MANAGER: GORDON GRIGGSBY

BBC, BARF, MONICA

Gordon Griggsby rubbed the brass plate with the sleeve of his suit and looked at his own (round) face beaming back at him.

Workmen hurried past him carrying counters and carpets and cabinets, taking tills and tiles inside, dragging desks and drawers and deed-boxes, and pots of paint and pictures for the walls of the halls, glass lamps and gas lamps, sliding-in signs and stools and banking tools (like pencils and pens and pots of ink for quires that the quills would quickly fill) and lifting the ledgers and carefully carrying those little sponge-things-the-clerks-use-to-wet-their-fingers. It was more like a beehive than a bank it was so bustlingly busy.

Cough!

Gordon Griggsby tightened his tie in the mirror of the brass plate and smiled at the round face that looked back. "Good morning, sir, and welcome to Withering's Wildpool bank. How may I help?" he asked himself.

Cough! Cough!

"Yes I will happily lend you money . . . and if you fail to pay me back I'll snatch your house and throw you out! Ha! Ha! Won't that be funny?"

101

Cough! Cough! Cough!

Gordon Griggsby suddenly realized a man was coughing. "Mr Griggsby . . . BBC, BARF, MONICA?" the man asked.

Griggsby kept the smile fixed on his round face and turned around. He saw a tall, thin man with shining brown skin and glowing green eyes looking at him. "Yes, sir? How may I help?"

The man reached inside his pocket and pulled out a business card.

Mr Samuel Preed
BBC, BARF, MONICA

Inspector

"Ah!" Gordon Griggsby cried. "A fellow member of the BBC?"

"The British Banking Corporation," Dreep nodded.

"And BARF."

"Bankers Association Royal Fellowship."

"And MONICA too."

"Member Of the National Institute of Chartered Accountants," Dreep agreed.

""How can I help a fellow banker?"

"As you see, I am an inspector. I have been sent by the BBC to make sure the building meets our standards."

"Oh, but it does!" the manager said smugly.

"The new standards – passed last week in London by BARF."

"Ah . . . oh . . . I didn't know about them," Griggsby said and the smile slid from his face like jelly off a wet plate.

"I will just have a quick look around, if you don't mind."

"Please, Mr Preed, let me show you this fine building," Griggsby cried and led the way inside.

Dreep pretended to be interested in the cash tills and the little barred windows, the desks where the clerks would sit and the tiny toilets they could use –

but no more than twice a day.

At last they reached the monstrous safe that stood in the back room like a silvery dinosaur with its door a gaping mouth. Workmen were bolting on the door. Dreep stepped inside. He tapped his foot on the wooden floor. It sounded as hollow as a wood floor should. He gave a thin smile.

Then he stepped outside the safe and walked around the room. The brick walls were bare. "Night safe," he said.

"Night safe?" Griggsby frowned.

"The shops of Wildpool close at around six o'clock in the evening. The bank closes at five. The shopkeepers can't pay in their money. They have to keep it in their shops overnight. That is dangerous."

"Dangerous?"

"There are so many criminals around," Dreep said in a low voice.

"So I've heard."

"Most banks have a 'night safe' . . . a hole in the wall where the shopkeepers can drop their money through . . . with a note to say who it's from, of course."

"Of course!"

"Now BARF says *every* new bank must have a night safe. Here is the design."

Dreep pulled out a plan.

BARF Standard Night Safe design

Door in the wall.
Door lock.
Chute
Collection box.

"It will be done by tomorrow," Gordon Griggsby said with a smile.

"I'll be back on Friday to test it and to collect a copy of the key. BARF keep copies of every night-safe key in the country, just in case some careless manager loses his key. Hah! But you wouldn't do that,

Mr Griggsby, would you?"

Griggsby laughed – roundly. "There is more chance of me losing every penny from my thief-proof safe!"

"Exactly!" Dreep cried. "You have a truly wonderful bank here, Mr Griggsby, and Wildpool is lucky to have a truly wonderful manager."

Dreep's fine white fingers rippled in a wave of goodbye.

Griggsby glowed, then a little crease of worry formed in the corner of his eyes. That wave. Those fine white fingers. There was something . . . something . . . not quite *right*.

He just couldn't work out what it was.

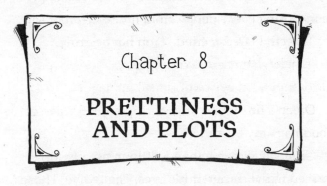

Chapter 8

PRETTINESS AND PLOTS

Samuel Dreep crossed the High Street to where Alice White sat with her match tray and her sign. He knew that despite his disguise, her clever criminal mind would recognize him.

NO MATCHES.

DON'T EVEN ASK.

JUST LEAVE YOUR MONEY.

I AM NOT BEGGING.

JUST ASKING POLITELY.

"Come back to Master Crook's Crime Academy, Alice," the teacher said. "Master Crook has your money put away safely. You don't need to beg."

The girl glared at him. "I am not begging."

"Then what are you doing?"

"Keeping an eye out."

"For what?"

"That's my business."

"Then at least come and sleep in the warm bedroom at the academy," Dreep sighed.

Alice jumped to her feet. "I am not sharing a room with Miss hoity-toity, namby-pamby, simpery-whimpery, high and mighty, pretty-witty, lardey-dardey, wishy-washy, snooty-snotty, goody-goody, burgling McGurgling Bunty!"

Samuel Dreep nodded slowly. "OK, there's plenty of room, but you still need to say sorry."

"I am *not* saying sorry! Alice White does not say sorry. Alice White does not know the meaning of the word. Alice White can't even spell the word and she certainly doesn't say the word."

"What word?"

"Sorry!"

"What word?"

"Sorry!!!"

"Apology accepted. Now come back to class,"
the teacher said. "We all miss you. Nancy has been
miserable since you walked out."

"Since I was *thrown* out."

"The Mixlys miss you . . . even Smiff misses you."

Alice took a deep breath. "I think I may be more
use here," she said quietly. "You'd be surprised what
you see, sitting on the corner."

Samuel Dreep leaned towards her. "What have you
seen, Alice?"

There was a gleam in her eyes as she said,
"Sparrows."

"What?"

"Good day, Mr Dreep. Tell dear Nancy I'll be back
as soon as Miss McGurgle is gone."

Friday 14th April 1837

Inspector Beadle's chair creaked.

*You would creak if you had his great bulk sitting on
you.*

He looked at his constables standing in front of his desk, their buttons shining silver, medals shining brass and faces shining with the rain of an April shower.

"The bank opens in three days' time," he said.

"Yes, sir, I can't wait to get some money out," Constable Larch said with a smile.

"Do you have money in Withering's bank?"

"No, sir."

"Then you can't get it out," the inspector explained.

"Can't I? I didn't know that," Larch said, disappointed.

"Not unless you go to Mr Griggsby and borrow money – but of course he will make you pay back a lot more than you borrow."

"That's not fair!" Larch complained.

"It's how banks work," the inspector said.

"I know how you can get money out of Withering's and not pay," thin Liddle said.

"How?"

"Rob it! Heh! Heh!"

"I'm glad you mentioned that, Liddle, because of course *now* is the time when thieves will be gathering

to spy on the bank," the inspector said. "Here are your orders for tonight."

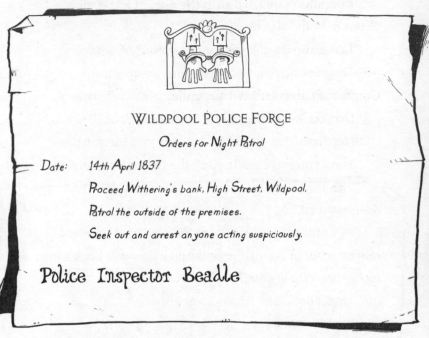

WILDPOOL POLICE FORCE

Orders for Night Patrol

Date: 14th April 1837

Proceed Withering's bank, High Street, Wildpool.

Patrol the outside of the premises.

Seek out and arrest anyone acting suspiciously.

Police Inspector Beadle

"Over the next few nights villains will be hanging around to look for weaknesses. Trying to find a way to rob the bank."

"We have our net guns!" Liddle said.

"They are for guarding the money wagons. We can't have officers on the streets with weapons like

that. You can be clumsy. You'll probably net Mayor Twistle!"

"It wouldn't be hard to catch him," Liddle moaned. "He's only the size of a gnome."

"Just go on patrol and keep a record of what you see. Dismissed."

"Yes, sir. Evenin' all!" the constables said. They saluted. They gathered their truncheons, handcuffs, dark lanterns and rattles and set off into the sunset.

WILDPOOL POLICE FORCE

Date: 14th April 1837

At eight p.m. Constables Larch and Liddle proceeded through the town to Withering's bank. A blind beggar sat in the doorway to the butcher shop chatting to a match girl. The beggar was told to proceed to Wildpool's wonderful workhouse. Constable Larch proceeded with him.

The girl said she was waiting for a tree to grow so she could chop it down and make some new matches. She then told Constable Liddle to shut his tatty moustached-mouth as there was something she wanted to see.

Constable Liddle saw a man proceed from the direction of Wildpool station and stop outside the house known as Master Crook's Crime Academy. He was a very respectable gentleman. He was the respectable gentleman who drove the money wagon, with a big beard, last Friday. (The man had the beard, not the wagon.)

The gentleman blew a whistle. A pupil from the school came to the gate and had a talk with him for about five minutes. "Aha!" the match girl said. "Just as I thought." But she wouldn't say what thought she thought that was just as she thought.

Several people proceeded past the bank when the taverns closed for the night. No one looked like a bank robber. But Constables Liddle and Larch agreed they do not know what a bank robber looks like as they have never seen one before. I mean a bank OR a bank robber.

Constables Liddle and Larch returned to the police station at eight a.m. daybreak for a cup of tea and a bowl of porridge (each).

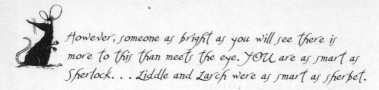

However, someone as bright as you will see there is more to this than meets the eye. YOU are as smart as Sherlock. . . Liddle and Larch were as smart as sherbet.

Alice heard the last three words that Silas Sharkle spoke to Bunty McGurgle as he walked back to the train station. "Same time tomorrow, Lottie."

Saturday 15th April 1837

Smiff marched into the police station. "Mr Dreep has lost his dog."

Constable Liddle took out a pencil and report sheet and asked, "What does he look like?"

"He's about six foot tall and always wears a top hat and a red-and-white striped scarf."

"A dog like that should be easy to spot!" Liddle cried.

"I think the young gent was describing Mr Dreep, Liddle," Larch said.

"Ah . . . so what's the dog like?" Liddle asked.

"Bones. He likes bones," Smiff told him. "And chasing cats."

"I meant what does he *look* like?"

"Four legs, a tail."

"He'd be easier to find if he had *five* legs," Larch sighed.

"Or a top hat and scarf," Liddle nodded. "What's his name?"

"Samuel . . . Samuel Dreep."

"Clever dog! Here! It's not that dog that's been on at the Apollo Music Hall this week, is it? Old Mother Hubbard's dog?"

"No," Smiff said.

"I want to go and see that show on my night off."

"When's that?"

"Sunday."

"It's a good show – the Fakir of Ava is wonderful," Smiff smiled. "If you are out on patrol you might spot him."

"The Fakir of Ava?"

"The dog. You may spot him."

"Aha!" Liddle cried and wrote on the form. "It's a spotted dog then."

"So," Smiff asked, "when will you be out on patrol? I mean, when can we expect a result?"

Constable Larch took a sheet from under the desk. Here you are," he said, showing the sheet to Smiff.

WILDPOOL POLICE FORCE
Duty Rota

Sunday 16th   Day off

Monday 17th   Liddle: Guard bank. Larch: patrol docks

Tuesday 18th   Liddle: Patrol taverns. Larch: guard bank

Wednesday 19th   Liddle: guard bank. Larch: patrol streets

Thursday 20th   Liddle: patrol posh houses. Larch: guard bank.

Friday 21st   Liddle: guard bank. Larch: patrol shops

Saturday 22nd   Liddle: check for beggars. Larch: guard bank

"See?" Larch said. "The villains never know where we'll be next. Our patrols are a closely guarded secret."

"Ah, but there is always someone guarding the bank," Smiff said.

"Yes. The mayor said that is the most important thing. It would be a terrible disgrace if we ever let the bank get robbed. In fact he would even take our medals off us."

"You wouldn't want that," Smiff said.

"We couldn't stop him."

"You could keep them in the bank!" Smiff said.

"Good idea!" Liddle and Larch cried. "Evenin' all," they called as the boy walked out.

Samuel Dreep shook his head. "So the bank is always guarded."

"Yes," Smiff said. "Except Sunday."

"Ah, but the money doesn't arrive till Monday."

"No point robbing an empty bank," Martin Mixly said.

"If Alice was here she would think of a way to get the constable away from the bank," Nancy said quietly.

"But Alice *isn't* here, sweetie," Bunty McGurgle said. "Still, the good news is you have me instead. I am twice as bright as her!"

"And twice as pretty," Smiff added.

"True," Bunty agreed.

"I remember the theft of the Twistle treasure," Smiff said. "Alice reported a crime at the *north* side of town and the constables went off to investigate – we did a robbery at the *south* side," Smiff said.

Samuel Dreep shook his head. "They won't fall for that trick again."

Bunty clapped her hands. "What about if Inspector

Beadle told the constables to leave the bank? They would *have* to go then."

Millie Mixly said, "Why would Inspector Beadle do that?"

"Because one of the rich men with money in Withering's bank would *tell* him to," Bunty said.

"We don't know any rich men with money in Withering's bank," Nancy said.

Bunty sat back in her chair and played with a curl. She looked as smug as a slug on a lettuce leaf. "I do," she said. "Remember Silas Sharkle?"

"Wasn't he the man that ruined your father and left you penniless?" Nancy asked.

"He was . . . but, to be honest it was Mr McGurgle's own greed that ruined him."

"Mr McGurgle?" Smiff asked. "You mean your dad?"

"Yes, sweetie, my Papa. Anyway, Silas Sharkle has another ship ready to sail. This one really is full of muskets and cannons, powder and bullets this time. What if I tell him someone is planning to set fire to the ship – some rebel Chinese plotters who don't want the weapons to go to China?"

Nancy tried to say, "How do you know about the

ship, Bunty?"

But her soft voice was drowned by the crow call of Smiff Smith. "Brilliant, Bunty! The police will go down to the docks and leave us free to get into the bank. Cor, Bunty, you really are twice as clever as Alice!"

"And twice as pretty," she agreed.

The blind beggar sat in the butcher's shop doorway, stroking his cat. He wondered where Alice the match girl was this evening.

Happy crowds strolled past on their way to the music hall or the taverns and happy people gave him happy coins. So everyone was happy.

High above Wildpool's gaslit glitter the town hall clock chimed the end of the day. *Ding-dong, ding-dong, ding-dong. . .*

A man walked from the railway station. The man was not tall but he seemed to fill the pavement. Crowds flowed round him like a stream round a rock. His eyebrows hung like curtains over his eyes and his beard was cut as square and heavy as a church door.

When he reached Master Crook's Crime Academy, he blew a whistle.

The door opened and a girl in a blue dress hurried to the shadow of the gate to meet him.

"Sign this," she said and passed him a letter.

Sharkle Mansions

Dear Constable Larch

As you know I deal in weapons. Weapons that defend our great British Empire. But our Empire has enemies! On Monday night of 17th April they plan to attack my ship in Wildpool harbour and burn it. There is enough gunpowder on board that ship to blow Wildpool into the North Sea.

These attackers are cowards. If they see two policemen on guard by the gangplank, they will not attack. The ship sails on Tuesday. I humbly ask that you send your brave constables to the docks on Monday night at midnight.

God save King William and the Empire.

Your humble servant,

"Why would I want to sign this, child?" the man asked.

"It will allow me to rob Withering's bank," she said.

"Remember all my valuables will be in there," he said quietly. "A hundred thousand pounds in bank notes and jewels. Do not take those."

"I know," she said. "But I will steal them and give them to you. Then Gordon Griggsby will be forced to pay you a hundred thousand pounds – or no one will ever use Withering's bank again."

"So I will have *two* hundred thousand pounds," the man nodded and a smile lit his eyes. "Clever child."

"Ah! But we can't allow the bank robbers to get away with a robbery," she said. "I will be first to leave the bank and I'll take with me all the Sharkle fortune. When you see me enter the bank send a second note to bring the constables up from the docks with their net guns. They will catch the whole gang."

The man shook his head. "They will catch *you*, child."

Bunty McGurgle sighed. "Of course you *tell* them you have a spy on the inside who must go free."

"How will they know you?"

"Just tell them to look out for the girl in the blue dress," she said.

"Clever. It's an evil plot."

"I'm an evil girl."

"Yes. Very clever. I double my money – and you? What is in it for you?"

"I am doing it to help my dear father, of course."

He nodded. "Pass me the paper to sign – there you are – Silas Sharkle!" he said.

When the man had walked back to the train station and the girl had slipped back into Master Crook's Crime Academy, a shadow moved in the shadow of the bushes. Alice White gave a grim grin. "All arrested? Serves them right I suppose. Should I warn them?" She stepped into the High Street and crossed between carriages to the butcher's shop. "Nah! Better let beautiful Bunty's plan go ahead."

"Hello there," the blind beggar said. "Where have you been?"

"Spying," Alice said.

The man rose and stretched and picked up his cat and his cap full of coins. "Time to make my way to the

workhouse," he said.

"The workhouse? Yes! That's just the place I need to be. I'll come with you."

"You can guide a poor, blind beggar," the man sighed.

"Hah!" Alice snorted. "That's what you have a guide-cat for. Now hurry up or we'll miss the plum pudding supper."

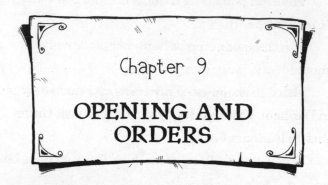

Chapter 9

OPENING AND ORDERS

Sunday 16th April 1837

Nancy Turnip walked back to Master Crook's Crime Academy from Wildpool church. She smiled because the vicar's message had been a happy one that Sunday morning. "The poor are blessed," he said.

Mayor Twistle had turned red and looked furious. "The poor are a nuisance," he'd muttered to his wife, Lady Arabella. But he muttered so loud half the church could hear him.

As Nancy walked through the gate and into the crime academy she heard her name called. "Oi! Nancy!"

The girl stopped and peered into the bushes. Alice White's thin face looked out and her thinner finger

beckoned. "Come here, Nancy! Come here, quick!"

"What are you doing there, Alice?" she asked. "Come inside."

"Nah! I'm not going back in that place while snooty-tooty, runty Bunty is there."

"I need to change into my boots and catch the coach to Darlham," Nancy said. "I'm going to visit Uncle Rick in Darlham Gaol."

"I know that," Alice sighed. "You *always* go there on a Sunday. *That's* why I need to talk to you. Before you go."

Nancy frowned. "Why?"

"Listen and I'll tell you," she said. Nancy hopped from foot to foot, knowing she hadn't time to stop and talk if she was going to catch the coach.

"There are a lot of villains in Darlham Gaol," Alice said.

For once Nancy's calm face creased crossly. "I know that, Alice. That's why they're in the gaol!"

Alice went on, "And villains know more about the rich than the rich know themselves. I want you to ask your Uncle Rick what he knows about Silas Sharkle."

"Silas Sharkle? Why?"

"It's a name I heard when I was spying. I want to know about his family. . ."

"But—" Nancy asked.

"Just do it," Alice snapped. "I am trying to save your miserable heads from the noose. Even Smiff who doesn't have a brain in that head of his. You have to trust me, Nancy." Her pale eyes stared hard at the crime academy pupil. "You do trust me, don't you?"

"Yes, Alice," Nancy said slowly.

"And find out if the prisoners know anything about the McGurgle family – and especially about their daughter Bunty."

"Are you doing this to get revenge on poor Bunty?" Nancy cried.

"I thought you trusted me," Alice hissed.

"I do, but—"

"Then don't ask questions," she said.

"You want me to go to Darlham Gaol."

"Yes."

"And ask questions."

"Yes."

"But you don't want me to ask questions."

"Right."

Nancy shook her head. Then the chimes of the town hall clock began to chime ten . . . *Ding-dong, ding-*

dong, ding-dong. . .

"I'll have to run!" Nancy moaned. "I'll be walking the streets of Darlham in my Sunday shoes. They'll be ruined."

"I'll buy you a new pair when this bank robbery's done."

Nancy hurried back into the High Street and Alice followed. "We have a brilliant plan to rob the bank," Nancy said.

"I can guess what it is," Alice said.

Nancy skidded to a halt. "You can?"

"Yes. And if I can work it out then so can the police."

"Constable Liddle and Constable Larch aren't that clever," Nancy said.

"No, but Inspector Beadle is. He's the one you have to watch. Him and Silas Sharkle."

Nancy hurried on. "Silas Sharkle . . . Silas Sharkle . . . I'll find out what I can," she promised.

The coachman was blowing a long horn to signal that the coach was about to leave. Nancy climbed up to an outside seat and turned up her collar against the cool breeze off the sea.

The rutted road threw up splashes of mud that marked Nancy's shining shoes. "I hope this is

important, Alice," she said to herself. "I hope it's important."

Alice watched the coach roll along the road to the south then turned and walked down Bridge Street to the bridge high over the Wildpool river. Even the shipyards below were steeped in a deep Sunday silence and only the wheeling seagulls' harsh cries disturbed her.

"Right, Alice White," she said as she looked down into the wind-whipped waves on the river. "You don't know why this Bunty McGurgle would want to help Silas Sharkle, do you? No you don't."

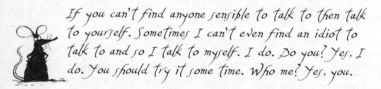

If you can't find anyone sensible to talk to then talk to yourself. Sometimes I can't even find an idiot to talk to and so I talk to myself. I do. Do you? Yes, I do. You should try it some time. Who me? Yes, you.

The tall walls of the Wildpool's Wonderful Workhouse loomed above her. The gates stood open, ready to welcome anyone unhappy enough to fall on hard times. They would be sure of a warm fire, a good meal and a bed here.

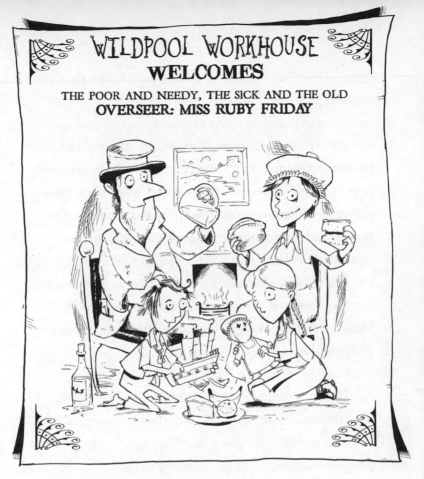

WILDPOOL WORKHOUSE
WELCOMES

THE POOR AND NEEDY, THE SICK AND THE OLD
OVERSEER: MISS RUBY FRIDAY

Families of children played happily in the courtyard. Alice marched through them with no time to stop and kick at the rag ball when it rolled in front of her.

Ruby Friday waited at the door and smiled at the girl. "Nice to see you, Alice. Come for a bed for the

night? There's always one here for you. Better than a cold shop doorway."

"Not this time. I've come to ask a favour, Miss Friday."

"Always ready to help Alice White. Most of the people in here will be gone in a month when their new houses are built. But we won't forget who helped that to happen," the overseer said. "You and your friends at Master Crook's Crime Academy."

"I'm not at the academy at the moment," Alice admitted.

"You still haven't made up your little argument then?"

"No. They still haven't said sorry to me," Alice sniffed. "But you and the workhouse people can help."

"Name it," Ruby Friday said.

"I want you to take the blue uniform material. . ."

"Plenty of that stuff," Ruby said. "We don't force our guests to wear workhouse uniforms any more."

Alice nodded. "It was a sign that you were a pauper – something to be ashamed of."

"So what do you want with it?" the overseer asked.

"I want your best dressmakers to take that material and make some clothes for me."

"Clothes? How many sets do you need?"

"Five should do it," Alice said. "I need five."

130

Monday 17th April 1837

The pupils of Master Crook's Crime Academy stood at the window and watched as a piece of paper was pasted over the sign.

They watched as Gordon Griggsby stood at the door. His smile shone as brightly as his bald head in the April sunshine. He threw open the doors. He welcomed in the new customers. He chatted brightly and shook hands.

From their window in the academy the pupils could see he often wiped his hand on the side of his long black coat – there were some hands that were dirty from more than money. Let that be a lesson to us all. I will not explain. You may be eating as you read this and I don't want you to throw up into your porridge.

The people of Wildpool stood in an eager queue. Some clutched purses and piggybanks, some carried bags and others just clung tight to their pockets.

"We'll leave a lot of people miserable," Nancy moaned. "Some of those poor people are putting everything they have in the bank!"

"You are right," Samuel Dreep said. "But inside the safe there are boxes that the really rich put their valuables in. We'll rob those."

"I think we should steal from just *one* box. The Silas

Sharkle box," Nancy said. "Uncle Rick in Darlham Gaol told me he is the richest."

"Sharkle is the man who robbed my father! Steal back the money and give it to me!" Bunty McGurgle said eagerly.

"I suppose we should give you the money Sharkle cheated your father out of," Dreep nodded at Bunty. "The rest is profit for Master Crook's Crime Academy . . . we share it out to the poor at the end of the year."

"If Master Crook's Crime Academy is still open at the end of the year," Bunty said softly to herself. "And if there are any pupils left to share it out."

Smiff didn't hear what she said. He just looked at her with a sickly smile – the sort of smile a rabbit has when it sees a bowl of carrots.

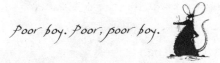

Poor boy. Poor, poor boy.

Silas Sharkle took a large key from his pocket and opened the heavy lid of the heavy chest that stood in his office at Darlham. Beside the chest stood a red box with gold lettering.

He began to lift bags of gold and silver, bundles of bank notes and boxes of coins out of the chest and put them in the red box.

"Ohhhh!" Mrs Sharkle muttered and fluttered. "I hate to see our money leave the house."

Silas Sharkle gave a grunt. "Foolish woman. It's not safe here. How would you like to wake up one night and find a gang of thugs breaking down our doors?"

"Gracious me, I wouldn't!" the woman whimpered.

"They *will* if they know I have McGurgle's hundred thousand pounds in the box."

"But you have the key, my love!" the woman said with a soft smile.

Silas Sharkle threw up his eyes till they disappeared into the hanging hedge of eyebrows. "They will simply carry off the whole box and smash it open when they get it back to their den."

"I never thought of that," his wife sighed. "I thought it would be safe. After all, no one knows it's here!" she said, feeling rather clever.

Her husband glared at her. "Ernest McGurgle knows it's here," he said quietly. "And if I were Ernest

McGurgle – penniless and desperate – I would gather a gang of the vilest villains in the country. I would send them to smash down our doors and rob us of our riches."

"Would he do that?" she gasped.

"That's what I would do if I were him," Sharkle snarled. "It's just a matter of time before McGurgle thinks of it – maybe he already has! So we don't just have to move our money to Withering's thief-proof safe, we have to let the whole world watch us as we do it. See?"

"Ooooh, you are so clever, Silas, ooooh," Mrs Sharkle said, cooing like a dove.

The man slammed down the lid on the chest and marched to the door. "There you are, constables! All ready to go! Take it to the waiting wagon."

Constables Liddle and Larch shuffled into the room. Liddle looked at Larch. "We can't lift a big chest like that!" Liddle cried. "Our orders say nothing about that!"

"Nothing!" Larch agreed and pulled out his orders.

WILDPOOL POLICE FORCE

Orders for Day Patrol

Date: 17th April 1837

Collect Net guns from Wildpool police station store cupboard.

Proceed to Sharkle Hall near Darlham.

Enter the premises. Escort the treasure chest on to the Withering's bank wagon.

Accompany the wagon to Helton station, sitting inside the vehicle. Beware highway robbers while crossing the moors. Warn the driver to stop for no one.

Escort the chest on to the Helton to Wildpool train, sitting inside the carriage. Beware train robbers while travelling to Wildpool. Warn Driver Rump to stop for no one.

Escort the chest on to the bank wagon from Wildpool station to the High Street. Beware gangs of wagon thieves and order the wagon driver to stop for no one — even girls lying down in the road.

Escort the chest into the safe and see it safely locked away.

Police Inspector Beadle

Sharkle snatched the paper. "No need to warn the wagon driver – it will be me."

"Sorry, sir, but it doesn't say nothing about lifting heavy chests," Liddle said.

"It says lots about hundreds of robbers trying to murder us!" Larch moaned.

"Ah, yes," Liddle nodded. "It's all right to get murdered . . . but it's not all right to hurt our old backs!"

"You're right," Larch agreed.

Silas Sharkle snapped, "I'll get the servants to carry it from here and the porters at the station."

As Sharkle left the room Liddle and Larch smiled at one another. "The public has to be told!" Liddle declared.

"Told what?" Larch asked.

"They can murder us as much as they like but they can't strain our backs," the proud policeman said.

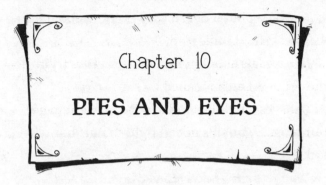

Chapter 10

PIES AND EYES

Samuel Dreep stood at the blackboard and ran through the plan one more time.

Master Crook's Crime Academy :
Secret Bank Robbery Plan
READ AND LEARN TELL NO ONE

MONDAY AND TUESDAY 17/18TH APRIL

11:30 p.m.   Streets empty after taverns and music hall close. Bunty approaches Constable Liddle on duty at Wildpool High Street. Gives him letter ordering him to join Larch at docks.

11:45 p.m.   Smiff, the Mixlys, Nancy and Bunty use Mr Dreep's key to open the night safe and climb into the bank. Mr Dreep (who is too big to fit) will pass through the tools and wait in the alley with the wheelbarrow. He will keep watch at the docks to make sure the constables stay there.

Midnight: Students remove the floorboards outside the safe. They dig into the earth and scoop out a tunnel under the safe. They saw through the floorboards inside the safe and climb in.

1:00 a.m.   Millie and Martin empty the Sharkle box and pass the loot to Smiff and Nancy who place it in "Swag" sacks. Bunty loads the wheelbarrow with the sacks.

2:00 a.m.   All return to Master Crook's Crime Academy.

"Any questions?" Mr Dreep asked.

"How will we know if the constables come back up to the High Street?" Smiff asked.

"I'll make sure I'm ahead of them. I'll whistle down the night-safe door and warn you to be quiet," Mr Dreep explained.

"But we'll be trapped inside," Nancy said.

"Not for long. Even if they stand guard all night the police night shift ends at eight in the morning. The bank doesn't open till nine. You have an hour to get clear."

"But the High Street will be busy by then," Martin Mixly argued.

"And all they will see is a couple of you wheeling a barrow with sacks across the road," the teacher explained. "But I'll do my best to get the constables away from the street – even if they do return. I'll think of something."

"The people in the High Street will see the tools – they'll know who did the robbery," Millie said.

"Leave the tools behind," Mr Dreep said.

"Then the police will check who bought those tools. The shopkeeper will remember me," Smiff said.

"If that happens we'll have to get you out of Wildpool to a safe town where no one knows you," the teacher promised.

"What!" Smiff wailed. "Away from Master Crook's Crime Academy, away from my Ma? Away from everyone?"

Bunty McGurgle patted Smiff on the arm. "It's all right, Smiff, I'll visit you."

Smiff gave his stupid rabbit smile and said, "That's all right then."

"Millie and Martin, have you told your parents

you'll be out for the night?" the teacher checked.

"Yes, sir . . . we said it's a school trip," Martin told him.

"And it is!" Millie chuckled.

"It'll be dark soon. Try to get some sleep," Samuel Dreep said. "And don't worry. Nothing can go wrong."

People have horrible accidents – they are run over by herds of mad pigs, crushed by falling pianos and drowned in tubs of treacle. And what are the last words most of these unfortunate people hear before they go to their dreadful deaths? You guessed it: "Nothing can go wrong."

Withering's bank wagon rolled down Wildpool High Street. Dozens of ruthless rogues watched and sighed. Hundreds of itching fingers wriggled.

Alice White sat on the corner of the High Street with a soft smile on her lips. Bank porters hurried out and lifted the red chest from the wagon. Two old constables climbed out, stiff as bank-window bars, and raised their fearsome net guns towards the waiting crowds.

142

The driver with a beard cut as square and as heavy as a church door climbed down and handed the reins to a servant who carried a rifle. "Take it away, Herbert."

"Yes, Mr Sharkle," the man replied and touched the front of his hat.

"I'm going in to see my money safely stowed away."

The chest vanished safely into the bank, Silas Sharkle followed and the doors slammed behind him.

Dozens of waiting faces fell in disappointment. "Gone, gone, gone," a woman in a fine satin dress sighed. "I suppose we'll have to find something easier to rob."

The crowd of villains nodded and trudged slowly back to Wildpool station.

One of them stopped on the corner and smiled at the thin girl who sat there with eyes as fiery as the setting April sun. "I'll have a box of matches for my pipe, my dear," the man said.

Alice White glared up at him. "Do I *look* like a match seller?"

"Well . . . yes. . ." and he glanced at her sign.

143

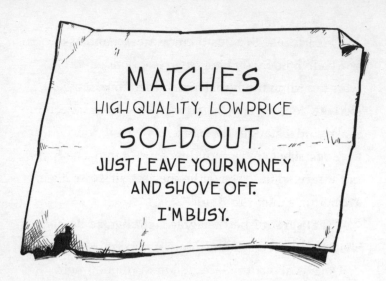

MATCHES
HIGH QUALITY, LOW PRICE
SOLD OUT.
JUST LEAVE YOUR MONEY
AND SHOVE OFF.
I'M BUSY.

"Pipe smoking is bad for you," Alice said. "You are better off without matches."

"I suppose so."

"I am doing you a favour by not selling you matches," she said.

"Thank you."

"Don't thank me – just pay me."

The man left sixpence and hurried off to the train station.

The constables hobbled over the road to Wildpool police station for a cup of tea and to have a rest before their night patrol started.

Inspector Beadle was there to meet them. "The plan worked, then. Everyone knew our brave constables were guarding the cash. No one tried to rob it. It's a job well done . . . a job *half* done. Now we just need to make sure it stays in the bank."

Constable Larch's round face broke into a happy, but weary, smile. "That's the easy bit, sir. Now it's in Withering's thief-proof safe."

"That's right," Liddle agreed and tugged on his wispy moustache to pull it out of the way of his tea. "Nothing can go wrong."

Mr Dreep checked his notes for the last time.

11:30 p.m.   Streets empty after taverns and music hall close. Bunty approaches Constable Liddle on duty at Wildpool High Street. Gives him letter ordering him to join Larch at docks.

The streets of Wildpool were never empty. The streets were lit by glowing gas lamps but the back alleyways were as dim as coal mines on the dark side of the moon.

145

And in those shadows the cats stalked the rats in a never-ending game of hide-and-seek.

Sometimes the cats caught the rats. Then it became a game of hide-and-squeak. Hah! Get it? Hide-and-squeak? Oh, dear, sometimes I'm so funny I could make a snake snigger.

The town hall clock struck eleven-thirty. *Ding-dong, ding-dong, ding-dong. . .*

Eleven-thirty didn't strike back.

This was the hour when burglars lurked.

This was the hour when children buried themselves under blankets to keep out the cold and to keep out spiky monsters that hid under beds to chew their toes.

This was the hour when the fine folk of Wildpool dined and wined. The hour when Mayor Oswald Twistle twirled his glass of port and passed a box of fat cigars to his rich guest.

"It's good of you to offer me a bed for the night, Sir Oswald," Silas Sharkle said.

Mayor Twistle was a small man, but no smaller than a gnome. His chest puffed out like a frog and his starched white shirt showed blotches of dropped dinner.

146

Steak pie in mushroom gravy, if you want to know.

"It is a pleasure," Mayor Twistle began. "No – it is an *honour* to welcome such a rich guest to my house. Nay, to the town of Wildpool. The town is richer for your visit. We have Withering's bank, of course, but what is a bank without a fortune in its thief-proof safe, eh?" he chuckled.

Sharkle stroked his beard and gave a sly smile. "I always take a walk after dinner, Sir Oswald," he said.

"I don't!" the little mayor squawked. "My feet hurt. It's these shoes, you know."

"No! No! No! Don't worry," Sharkle said swiftly. "I like to walk alone. It helps me sleep. I thought I'd take a stroll by the bank tonight."

"Ahhhh! You'll see one of our brave constables on guard there. Our constables have medals for their gallant acts you know?"

"I know. You're lucky to have such fine fellows," Sharkle said. He let the butler help him put on a dark cloak and he walked out into the quiet road that led towards Wildpool town centre.

When he reached the High Street he stood in the

shadow of a shop doorway. He watched a girl in a blue dress pass a note to a thin policeman. In the breeze he heard the policeman read it slowly.

"Deal in weapons . . . our Empire has enemies . . . plan to attack my ship in Wildpool harbour . . . blow Wildpool into the North Sea . . . two policemen on guard by the gangplank they will not attack . . . send your brave constables to the docks on Monday night at midnight . . . God save King William and the Empire. Ooooh!" The constable groaned. "Inspector Beadle says I have to guard the bank."

"Guard what?" Bunty McGurgle laughed. "Who on earth is going to break into a bank when everything is locked away in a thief-proof safe."

"That's true. And if we don't stop the Chinese plotters Wildpool will be blown into the North Sea," the policeman groaned. "I have to stay and I have to go. What do I do?"

"It's a fine medal you have there, Constable," the girl said.

"The best I've ever seen," Constable Liddle said and spat on it before rubbing it with his sleeve.

"Imagine the size of the medal you'll get when

you save the whole of Wildpool! It will be the size of a dinner plate. It will be amazing. You will be Wildpool's greatest hero!"

"I will!" Liddle cried and he hurried off to Low Street and down to the quayside.

The girl in the blue dress smiled and rubbed her hands. The man in the dark cloak smiled and rubbed his hands. "Nothing can go wrong," he said.

From an even deeper and darker doorway, Alice White clutched at a soft bundle in her arms. She watched and waited.

She saw Bunty McGurgle wave a hand. Samuel Dreep stepped out from the gateway of Master Crook's Crime Academy. He trotted to the top of Low Street to make sure the constable was on his way. He waved back to the gateway. Four pupils from the academy stepped out with a wheelbarrow. The teacher checked his notes.

11:45 p.m. Smiff, the Mixlys, Nancy and Bunty use Mr Dreep's key to open the night safe and climb into the bank. Mr Dreep (who is too big to fit) will pass through the tools and wait in the alley with the wheelbarrow. He will keep watch at the docks to make sure the constables stay there.

Alice saw the pupils run across the road and disappear into the alley that ran by the side of the bank. She heard a key clink in the door to the night safe. *Clink.* "Careless," she muttered.

She heard muffled groans as one by one the pupils slid into the gap. She saw Mr Dreep run back and heard clanging of spades and pick-axes ratting on the iron door frame. *Clang.* "Ooooh!" she said to a passing rat. "If I'd been there I'd have wrapped those tools in sacking to muffle the sound."

"Squeak," the rat agreed.

At least I think the rat agreed. My rat-speak isn't too good. The rat could have said, "Excuse me but could I buy a box of matches?" Luckily for the rat Alice's rat-squeak-speak wasn't very good either or it would have been (a) rat, then (b) splat.

The great Wildpool bank robbery was under way. The robbery so secret no one should have been watching. But, in truth, eight eyes were watching the robbers' raid.

Oh, dear.

Chapter 11

MIDNIGHT AND MESSAGE

Alice White waited. She knew it would take at least forty to fifty minutes for them to break through the floorboards and reach the money. Even with Nancy-the-strong working her hardest.

Silas Sharkle waited. He knew it was no use calling the policemen back to catch the thieves until the girl in the blue dress had escaped with his fortune.

Samuel Dreep waited. He knew the class could do the job. He only wished Alice White was in there to drive them on. He watched the hands on the town hall clock creep round to midnight. His wavering fingers twitched at his notes.

Another pair of eyes watched and waited.

Who could that be? you cry. I'm not telling you, I cry back. Wait and see or work it out from the clues I've given you. Clues? you cry. Now stop all this crying or you'll make the pages damp.

Midnight chimed.

Mr Dreep was sure the constables were on the quayside. He took time to walk back up the High Street to check the alley at the side of the bank.

He could hear the sound of the class working but it was too early for them to be passing out the treasures. The teacher walked close to the doorway where Silas Sharkle was standing in shadow.

Sharkle stepped back so the teacher wouldn't see him. He stepped on to something soft but crunchy. "Hey! Watch where you're putting your shiny boots!" a voice groaned . . . the voice of that fourth pair of eyes. The voice of Wildpool's blind beggar.

"Who are you?" Sharkle hissed.

"I'm a very disturbed beggar," the man said. "Who are you?"

Sharkle's smile glittered in the little light there was. "I am your best friend," he said. "And you are going to help me. You're just what I need."

"I am?"

"You are." He pushed a hand into a pocket of his jacket and pulled out an envelope. "I have a message here I need delivered."

"At this time of night?" the beggar asked.

"Yes. I want you to go down to the docks and give it to the captain of a ship called the *Guns of Doom*."

"You what?" the beggar cried. "I'm not going down to the docks in the dark. There's all sorts of rogues hiding in lots of back alleys just waiting to jump out and rob you. I'm scared of the dark."

"You're blind!" Sharkle argued. "It's always dark to you."

153

"So I'm always scared. You wouldn't get me going to those docks . . . not for ten shillings, you wouldn't."

"What about for a guinea?" Sharkle asked and jingled some coins.

"I'm your man!" the beggar said and he was on his feet faster than a cat after a rat.

"Here's the money and here's the note." The clock chimed quarter-past midnight. "Time to go," Silas Sharkle said.

The beggar set off towards Low Street. Sharkle shrugged himself inside his cloak and set off back to his comfortable bed in Mayor Twistle's house. He knew the plan would be safe in the hands of the girl in a blue dress.

Mr Dreep hurried back to the end of the High Street. He looked down Low Street to watch for police. He saw the back of the blind beggar hurrying down the steep, cobbled street.

Now there was just one pair of eyes peering at the alley by the side of the bank – Alice White's.

She decided it was time for her to make her move.

*

Inside Withering's bank, the class worked steadily – but noisily. Floorboards splintered and were thrown against the wall, shovels crunched into the stony soil and earth was scattered over the floor. From time to time a shovel struck the side of the thief-proof safe and it rang like a gong.

At last the tunnel was large enough to let Nancy slip in. She pushed up on the floor inside the safe. She sweated and strained and gasped and gurgled. At last there was a cracking sound and Nancy croaked, "Done it!"

She hammered at the broken boards with her fists and soon the gap was large enough to let her climb up into the safe. "Pass me a candle," she panted.

The flickering amber light shone on a wall of brass doors. Behind each door was a box and in most of the boxes lay someone's precious parcel of savings or something worth its weight in yellow gold.

Smiff was next through the tunnel. He looked at the brass. Each had a small label in a slot. "Here we are."

Property of
Mr Silas Sharkle
Only to be opened by
the authorised owner
of Key.
Safety deposit box
number
39

"Can you open it?" Nancy asked.

Smiff Smith nodded. "Yes. They just have simple locks on these boxes. Gordon Griggsby never expected thieves to get this far, did he?"

As Smiff set to work to pick the lock, Millie and Martin Mixly slipped through the opening. "Where's Bunty?" Nancy asked.

"Waiting on the other side to pull the treasure through," Millie explained.

"She said she'll be fine, waiting there alone," Martin said. "It would spook me!"

"Nothing can happen to her," Nancy said. "There's no one there."

Hah! That's what you think, dear Nancy.

Alice White crossed the quiet High Street with a bundle over her shoulder.

She walked down the alley by the side of the bank. She stepped carefully past the wheelbarrow that stood there. She gently pushed the night-safe door open.

She looked through. A single candle lit the room. The massive thief-proof safe shone like polished silver.

A girl sat on a pile of sacks. She was looking at a hole in the floor that led under the wall of the safe. She had her back to Alice.

"Careless sort of look-out, Bunty McGurgle," Alice said softly to herself. "You haven't learned much from your time at Master Crook's Crime Academy. I will also show you how to get through an iron door

without the sort of racket you lot made."

Alice moved so smoothly through the gap she was inside in a silent moment. She pulled the soft bundle after her. The bundle was fastened at the top with a thin rope. She tugged the knot and the rope came loose.

A bundle of blue tumbled on to the floor. Alice took the rope and held one end in each hand. Then she stepped softly over the soil-stained floor till she was standing behind the girl in the blue dress. "No more burgling McGurgling," she said with a fierce smile.

Constable Larch saw a sinister shape creeping along the quayside. "Halt or I will beat you with my truncheon till you are black and blue – well a nasty shade of pink anyway. Who goes there?"

"It's me, Liddle," his partner said.

"Evenin' all. Aren't you supposed to be guarding the bank?"

"New orders." Liddle explained quickly. "Wildpool will be blown away if we don't stop these plotters. *Boom!*"

"Better get to the *Guns of Boom* then," Larch

croaked. "We could get hurt if Wildpool gets blown away."

The men marched down the quayside. The fish filleters had gone home to supper – fish pie with fried fish and fish pudding with fish custard. The dock workers had unloaded their last sacks of the day and the sailors were supping in the taverns. Only the ship-builders went on hammering to finish the mighty, the new, steel steam-ship that would be one of the first in the world. It was called *The Pride of Wildpool*.

The ship named *Guns of Doom* lay at the quay with a shaky gangplank to the shore. A man in a thick blue jumper and cap stood at the top of the plank.

"Evenin' all," the constables said. They placed themselves at the bottom of the plank and peered left and right along the quayside. Larch took a pie from his pocket and started to munch it. Gravy ran down his chin.

After a minute the sailor called, "Can I help you?"

"We've been sent to guard your ship," Liddle explained.

"Why?" the seaman asked.

"Our information says there may be an attack from

Chinese enemies," Larch said. "But, fear not! We will make sure you're safe!"

"Does my captain know about this attack?" the seaman asked.

"Maybe not," Liddle said. "It's a secret."

"I'd better tell him," the seaman said.

"What's his name?"

"Hoo," the seaman replied.

"The *captain*. Who is he?"

"Yes," the seaman said.

Liddle muttered to Larch, "I think we are dealing with an idiot here."

"Oh, yes. I know an idiot when I meet one," Larch nodded.

Of COURSE Larch knew an idiot when he saw one. Because he saw one every time he looked in the mirror.

"What's your name?" Liddle asked the seaman.

"Watt," the man said.

"I said what's your name."

"That's right. It is."

"What?"

"Yes."

Liddle sighed. "Yes. Mad as a March hare."

Larch frowned. "What? In April?"

Liddle looked at his partner and wondered if he was talking to TWO idiots. He turned back to the seaman. "I'm Liddle."

"Well . . . you're thin but you're quite tall. I wouldn't call you little."

Liddle went on, "And my partner is Larch."

"Maybe he shouldn't eat so many pies," the seaman said. "I'll go and report to my captain."

"What?"

"No, that's me. Hoo is the captain."

"I don't know . . . we've been asking you for ages."

"I'm a little confused," the sailor sighed.

"No. I'm not confused," Liddle said. The sailor disappeared. "Idiot. I'm surprised they don't crash their ship."

"Oh, but they do! I read in the *Wildpool Gazette* that Silas Sharkle lost a ship last month. The captain said he was lucky to escape alive."

"Well he couldn't escape dead, could he?" Liddle

grumbled. "It was probably the same captain. What was his name?"

"Hoo."

"The captain."

Larch stared at the thin constable. He pushed the rest of his pie in his mouth. "Forget it."

"What?"

"I think that was the name of the lieutenant. Now keep your eyes open for Chinese villains," Larch said.

"What does a Chinese villain look like?" Liddle asked.

"I'm sorry you asked me that, Liddle."

"Why?"

"Because I don't know the answer. But if *anyone* comes down Low Street firing pistols just hit them with your truncheon."

"Here's one now!" Liddle cried. "Halt! Who goes there?"

"Blind beggar," the man said.

"Shouldn't you be in the workhouse?" Larch asked.

"Just dropping off a message for the captain, then I'll be on my way," the beggar explained.

"An odd time to be delivering messages," Liddle said.

"That's what I said to the bloke that gave me the message," the beggar agreed. "But he said it was important. Fella in a cloak."

"A cloak? Sounds like a plotter to me. Did he look Chinese?"

"I don't know, it was dark. Anyway, I'm blind."

"Better look at that note," Larch put in.

"Careful!" Liddle called. "It could be an exploding letter!"

"Is it an exploding letter?" Larch asked the beggar.

"Let's find out," the man said. He took the letter and placed it on the cobbles. Then he jumped on it with his heavy boots.

Nothing. No *boom*. Not a sound – well, maybe a little rustle.

This is a foolish way to test for exploding letters, of course. If YOU ever get an exploding letter do NOT jump up and down on it. Place it on a gravestone in a churchyard, climb the church steeple and throw rocks down till you hit the letter. Duck out of the way of flying bones and you should be fine.

The beggar handed it over. "Safe as Withering's bank," he said.

Liddle read it in the dim light of the quayside lamps.

Captain Ping Hoo
If two police officers turn up at the ship tell them it's a trick. They must go straight to the police station, get their net guns and guard the bank. There is a robbery taking place. If the criminals are already inside the bank then they must capture them as they try to escape.

They must not net the girl in the blue dress. She is an insider.

A friend

"Ohhhh!" Liddle moaned. "We've been tricked! We could lose our medals if Withering's bank gets robbed."

"Ooooh! But that letter could be a trick to get us

away from the ship we were sent to guard!" Larch cried. The two officers ran in small circles wondering what to do next.

Captain Hoo and seaman Watt came on deck to see what was going on.

"No!" Liddle said suddenly. "No, no, *no*! The letter is NOT a trick."

"How do you know?" Larch moaned.

"Because, Larch, it was signed by 'a friend' . . . and a friend wouldn't try to trick us!"

"Brilliant, Liddle. You're right! Let's get to the bank before we lose our medals."

The officers shook their rattles to scare dogs and rats and cats out of the way as they hurried up Low Street towards the bank.

The captain of *Guns of Doom* shook his head. "What an idiot."

The seaman snapped, "How dare you!"

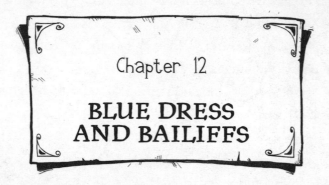

Chapter 12

BLUE DRESS
AND BAILIFFS

Tuesday 18th April 1837

"Hello, Charlotte," Alice said.

The girl in the blue dress gave a small scream and swung round. "Alice! You gave me a fright. What are you doing here? You've been expelled."

"Not exactly. I was sent away till I apologized to Bunty McGurgle," she said with a little sadness in her voice.

"If you are ready to apologize then I accept your apology. You can stay and help if you like."

Alice shook her head. "You are too kind. You would like that, wouldn't you?"

"Well," the girl said, "if you are truly sorry you are welcome to share in the robbery."

Alice nodded. "And share in the punishment when everyone is caught?"

"Why do you say that? I was just trying to show you are forgiven. You apologized. . ."

"To Bunty McGurgle, not to you," Alice said.

"But I am Bunty McGurgle!" the girl in the blue dress said.

"No, you are Charlotte Sharkle . . . your father calls you Lottie. A friend in Darlham asked questions about you. Bunty McGurgle has red hair – yours is dark brown like your father's. I'm sure your beard will grow like your father's one day."

The girl turned fiercely on Alice. "You will pay for that you little slabberdegullion."

"Pay for it? When I'm caught by Wildpool police?" Alice asked. "The police your father sent for once we were all trapped inside the bank?"

"Yes," Charlotte Sharkle sneered. There was a rattle behind her and a sack marked "Swag" was pushed through the hole in the floor. Charlotte snatched it and threw it through the night-safe door so it landed next to the wheelbarrow in the side alley. She came back for the next sack. Alice smiled. "That's very kind of

you. Loading the McGurgle fortune so we can wheel it away."

"You won't get away," the dark-haired girl said as the third heavy sack appeared from the safe. She carried it across the floor and sent it to join the others.

"Don't tell me – we will all be hanged while you wheel the treasure away."

"That's right," Charlotte Sharkle said.

The fourth and last bag marked "Swag" appeared and the girl carried it across to the door and threw it out.

Moments later Nancy wriggled out of the tunnel followed by the Mixly twins and finally Smiff.

"What are you doing here?" Smiff asked. "Don't tell me – you've betrayed us out of spite?"

"No," Nancy said quickly. "Alice is saving you." She looked around the group. "Alice got me to ask about the McGurgle and Sharkle families when I was visiting Uncle Rick in gaol. This girl here is Charlotte Sharkle – she's helping to steal her own father's money."

"Oh, so it was *you* that spied for Alice in Darlham, was it? I expect nothing less from a frumpy, ugly

serving girl."

"It's not true, Bunty, is it?" Smiff cried. "Alice is lying because she's jealous of your pretty face."

Charlotte Sharkle sighed. "Of course it's true, you stupid little, weedy little gutter child."

"I thought you *liked* me!"

"Hah! Like a slum boy? I think not."

Smiff slumped against the shining safe. His hurting eyes turned to Alice. "Sorry, Alice," he muttered.

She shrugged. "Charlotte Sharkle is a good actress," she said. "She even fooled Mr Dreep. Nothing to be ashamed of, Smiff."

"The best actress in my school," Charlotte gloated.

Before anyone could answer there was a low whistle from the night-safe door. "The police!" Smiff cried. "That's the signal. The police are here! We're done for."

"Yes you are, slum boy," Charlotte said. "But I'll be fine."

"You're part of the robbery. You'll hang alongside us," Millie Mixly said angrily.

"I think not. You see, I have something you don't have," Charlotte Sharkle said.

"A rich father?" Nancy asked.

"No something much simpler. A blue dress." And she laughed.

Samuel Dreep had seen the two constables appear at the bottom of Low Street. They seemed to be hurrying as fast as their old legs would carry them.

The town hall clock struck one. Dreep knew what the notes said.

1:00 a.m.   Millie and Martin empty the Sharkle box and pass the loot to Smiff and Nancy who place it in "Swag" sacks. Bunty loads the wheelbarrow with the sacks.

The class would be caught loading the loot from the bank. The policemen seemed to be carrying their net guns. Even if they only caught one pupil each it would be a disaster. The teacher ran ahead of the police and turned into the alley at the side of the bank. He stumbled over the sacks on the ground and heaved them into the wheelbarrow.

He placed his face to the night-safe door and whistled.

171

He waited.

Nothing happened. He could hear them talking. But no one was making a run for freedom.

Samuel Dreep looked back towards the gaslit street. The constables appeared. A half-moon made shadows in the alley. He shrank back into one of the shadows so the constables couldn't see him. Whichever pupil came out now they would be captured. He moaned. "Master Crook would know what to do – even *Alice* thinks quicker than me. I wish they were here!"

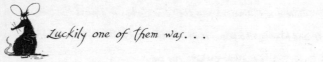

Luckily one of them was. . .

Alice White, inside the bank, heard the whistle but did not panic. "Yes, Charlotte Sharkle, you have a blue dress. And, as it happens, I have another five blue dresses here," she said nodding to her bundle. "A good friend made them for me. Four small ones for the Mixlys, me and Smiff. And a . . . er . . . slightly larger one for Nancy. We will put them on and walk free."

Charlotte Sharkle's face twisted in rage. "Clever little slabberdegullion, aren't we? But even if you walk

free with Papa's money he'll get it all back from the bank."

"Maybe," Alice said with a wide smile. She passed the dresses around the class.

"I'm not wearing a dress," Smiff Smith objected.

"That's fine, Smiff. Part of your dear Charlotte's plan is to bring the constables here to arrest us. You heard Mr Dreep whistle. They're waiting for you now. If you're not wearing a blue dress they'll arrest you."

"They won't catch me," the boy muttered. "I'll outrun two old coppers."

"We tried that, Smiff," Nancy said. "But we couldn't outrun the net-guns."

Martin Mixly said, "I don't mind wearing a dress if it saves me from the gallows," and he slipped one over his head.

"You look stupid," Smiff snapped.

"Yes, but at least he looks stupid on the streets of Wildpool . . . at night where there's no one to see him," Millie said as she put her dress on. "*You'll* be looking stupid on the gallows outside Darlham Gaol!"

"But we'll all come along to watch, Smiff," Alice promised. "We'll wave to you!"

The thin boy snatched the dress from Alice and pulled it over his head. "Right. Can we go now?"

"Oh, no!" Alice cried. "There's one more thing we need to do. We need to let the constables arrest *someone* for the robbery. We want them to keep their jobs, don't we?"

"But we're *all* wearing blue dresses," Millie argued.

"I've thought of that," Alice said. "Martin and Millie, hold Charlotte Sharkle's arms so she can't move. Nancy, hold her legs so she can't kick out – that's right. Now what have we here at the bottom of my bundle? Why it's a pot of paint and a brush. Red paint. Now, Charlotte, hoity-toity, namby-pamby, simpery-whimpery, high and mighty, lardey-dardey, wishy-washy, snooty-snotty, goody-goody, burgling bungler – we'll have you red as a rose in no time!"

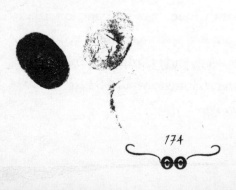

WILDPOOL POLICE FORCE
Report

Date: 18th April 1837

Constables Larch and Liddle proceeded to Withering's bank, acting upon information received in a letter.

We proceeded to the night safe in the alley at the side of the bank. The door was open. We observed a wheelbarrow with sacks marked "Swag" outside the safe door.

After a while the head of a boy appeared from the safe. However we were mistaken. He was wearing a dress so he could not have been a boy. We had been instructed not to arrest a girl in a blue dress so we did. That is to say we did un-arrest her. The girl said, "Evening all," then walked towards the High Street.

A second boy who looked like a girl emerged in a blue dress. We un-arrested her as well.

Two thin girls in blue dresses (who looked like girls) emerged. We un-arrested them. Then a large girl in a blue dress emerged. She took the heavy wheelbarrow and wheeled it away. Then a girl in a red dress emerged. She said it was a blue dress but Constables Larch and Liddle are not easily fooled. We arrested her. She screamed very loudly about being a shark, but that is a fish and we are not easily fooled. Fish don't wear red dresses.

The girl in the red dress was locked in the cell to cool off. We gave her no blankets to help her do so. Inspector Beadle will question the suspect.

Smiff Smith's mother had hair like a bird's nest. Some people in Low Street swear they saw the odd family of sparrows flying in and out of it.

This was a cruel lie made up by jealous people. Let me put the record straight. I was there and I know it wasn't true. Mrs Smith did NOT have a family of sparrows nesting in her hair. Definitely not. They were starlings.

The Master Crook's Crime Academy students and Mr Dreep sat around Mrs Smith's kitchen table. They were silent.

The money from Silas Sharkle's safe-box was stacked on the table. Mrs Smith had made a list.

The Sharkle fortune	
Pennies	£10,00,00
Florins	£10,00,00
Half Crowns	£80,00,00
Sovereigns	£900,00,00
5 bank notes	£99,000,00,00
Bank draft	£10,000,00,00
TOTAL	£110,000,00,00

"One hundred and TEN thousand pounds," Smiff breathed.

"One hundred and *ten*?" Millie Mixly echoed. "I thought he robbed Mr McGurgle of just a hundred thousand."

"Where did the extra ten thousand come from?" Alice asked.

Mr Dreep spread his rippling fingers. "Who cares? We know where it is going *to*. That ten thousand pounds is going into the Master Crook's Crime Academy treasure chest to be shared out to the poor at Christmas."

"And the hundred thousand?" Martin said, his eyes fixed on the piles of money on the table.

"We have all agreed on where that will go," Samuel Dreep said.

None of the eyes left the shining pile. All of the heads nodded.

Bunty McGurgle sniffed back tears. "So, Daddy? I will have to leave Darlham Ladies College?" she asked in a voice like a mouse – a very unhappy mouse.

I am talking about the real Bunty McGurgle here, not Charlotte Sharkle pretending to be Bunty McGurgle. Not Bunty McGurgle pretending to be Charlotte Sharkle . . . though I don't know why she would want to do that. No, this is Bunty McGurgle being herself. Got that? Good.

"Yes, my little Bunty-wunty. Daddy lost all his money when the ship sank in the China Sea."

"Two sugars please," Bunty said.

"Pardon?"

"If you're making some China tea I'll have a cup with two sugars, please," the girl sighed with a mousy sigh.

"China *Sea* . . . Silas Sharkle's sip shank . . . I mean ship sank. We are left with nothing."

"Nothing, Daddy? Not even a cup of China tea?"

"Not even a cup. Today the bailiff will arrive and take away our every possession. Darlham workhouse is a harsh place, Bunty, but it's what your foolish Daddy deserves."

"I thought a bay leaf was a herb you put in a stew, Daddy," Bunty said with a frown on her pale face.

"No, my little cherub, I said *bailiff*, not *bay leaf*.

178

The bailiff is a man who takes our things and sells them to pay the people we owe money to. He can take everything we have except the clothes we are wearing."

"Will Charlotte Sharkle and her parents lose everything too?"

Mr McGurgle pushed back his thin hair . . . hair that was turning grey with worry.

Hair does that you know. It turns grey with worry. But don't YOU worry about your hair turning grey. It can also turn blue, green, pink or black with hair dye. Buy some at your local apothecary shop as soon as you spot a grey hair.

"No. Mr Sharkle said his ship was insured – an insurance company paid him ten thousand pounds for the sunken ship. It was the weapons I bought that were not insured."

"Are the bay leafs very nasty men?" Bunty trembled.

There was a rattle on the door.

"We'll soon see," Mr McGurgle said. "That'll be them now."

Chapter 13

KNOCKING
AND NOTHING

Gordon Griggsby looked at the wrecked room where the thief-proof safe stood. His round face trembled with rage. "It was that man, Preed – he told me to build that night-safe door – and *he* had a key. It was all part of a cunning plot."

He looked at Constable Liddle who had broken the news of the robbery to him. "The bank will pay for posters of this man all over the country. Find *him* and we'll find our money."

By the end of morning those posters were printed.

WANTED
DEAD OR ALIVE

MR PREED

BANK ROBBER
£10,000 REWARD

Constable Liddle lifted his hat and scratched his head. "Strange that only the Sharkle box was opened. Maybe the gallant actions of me and Larch stopped her before she got away with more."

Gordon Griggsby peered up at the constable and spoke very slowly. "It is VERY strange that only the Sharkle box was touched. An interesting point, constable."

"It takes a wise dog to fool Wildpool Police, Mr Griggsby, sir. We have medals you know."

Griggsby frowned. "And you say you have one of the gang under arrest?"

"Yes, sir."

"But you didn't get the money?"

"No, sir."

"Then let's go and pay this bank robber a visit. See what he has to tell us before they hang him."

"She, sir. It's a young lady in a red dress."

"A girl, eh?" Griggsby said. "Very interesting. Inspector Beadle is known to me. He won't mind if I am in the room while you torture the villain and get her to confess."

Constable Liddle gasped. "Ooooh! Sir! We never

torture no one! We sometimes makes them eat one of Mrs Bunton's meat pies. That's a bit cruel. But we never hurts them!"

"I'll hurt her if I don't get my money back," Griggsby growled. "Withering's bank trusts me. I will not let them down."

Charlotte Sharkle was shivering and smudged with red paint. "I am Charlotte Sharkle and I demand to be released," she said to Inspector Beadle. The large policeman sat at a desk . . . in a very strong chair.

"So you say," the bald, round bank manager said. He sat alongside the inspector and glared at the girl through his spectacles.

Inspector Beadle nodded. "This is Mr Gordon Griggsby, manager of Withering's bank – the bank that you robbed last night."

"It wasn't me."

"The constables caught you coming out of the night-safe door," the inspector reminded her. "The Sharkle safe-box was empty. The box that contained over a hundred thousand pounds. Now you say you are Silas Sharkle's daughter."

"I *am*!" she cried. "Papa is staying with Mayor

Twistle – go and ask him. He'll tell you."

"Tell us what? That you are his daughter? Or that *he* is part of the plot to rob Withering's bank?" Gordon Griggsby asked. "Because, if he *is*, then he'll hang beside you on Darlham gallows! No one robs my bank and gets away with it! Clever Constable Liddle *said* it was odd that only the Sharkle box was robbed. Now we know why."

Inspector Beadle held up a huge hand. "Let's send for Mr Sharkle and see what he has to say." The inspector sent the weary old Constable Liddle up to South Drive to bring Silas Sharkle to Wildpool police station. "Constable Larch can make us a pot of tea while we wait."

"Yes, that would be nice. Two sugars," Charlotte sighed.

"Water for the prisoner," Inspector Beadle said.

Bunty McGurgle – the real Bunty McGurgle – walked to the front door with her father.

She looked out to see the bailiff. Would he be as strong as an ox and as wild as a wasp? Or as wild as an ox and strong as a wasp.

Bunty stared. Bunty's little mouth flew open. A gasp flew out of it. "Look, Daddy! Look!"

"I'm looking. I see it. I don't believe it."

For there . . . there on the McGurgle doorstep . . . stood no one. No one at all.

"Is someone playing knocky-nine-doors with us?" Bunty asked.

"I don't think bailiffs do that," her father said. "I thought I saw two children running away."

"What are these bags on our doorstep? Someone left them there, knocked then ran away. Who would do such a thing? Daddy, oh Daddy!" Bunty cried in her mouse-squeak voice.

"Yes, Bunty-wunty. Who would do such a thing?"

"Daddy, oh Daddy . . . I haven't a clue."

"Oh. Better go back inside and wait for the bailiff to arrive."

Mr McGurgle closed the door.

"Daddy?"

"Yes, Bunty-wunty?"

"Do you think we should open the sacks? They were marked 'Swag', is that like loot? Miss Meldrum said a lute is something the Ancient Greeks used to

play. She told us a lovely story about Orpheus who played his lute for his girlfriend. And then she was poisoned by Charlotte Sharkle."

"Orpheus's girlfriend was poisoned by Charlotte Sharkle?"

"No, Daddy . . . Miss Meldrum was poisoned by Charlotte. Can we open them, Daddy? I've always wanted to see a real lute."

Orpheus and his lute is a famous Greek myth – or maybe it was a "lyre". My teacher said Orpheus played a "lyre" – he played so beautifully he could turn iron soft and melt stones. But I think my teacher was a lyre.

Go ahead, Bunty," the man said and opened the door.

Bunty untied the first sack and sobbed. "Oh, no! Oh how disappointing!"

"No lute?"

"No, just a bag stuffed with money," Bunty McGurgle sighed. "Oh, I am sad."

"Money? How much?"

"Don't know, Daddy. About a hundred thousand pounds . . . at a guess."

Inspector Beadle sat at the desk. Gordon Griggsby sat beside him.

At the other side of the desk sat the red-painted Charlotte Sharkle and her father.

For a long while the only sound in the room was the ticking of the clock. For every tick there was a tock of the clock. And so it went on. Finally Silas Sharkle spoke. His beard rustled against his hard, white collar.

"Withering's bank lost my hundred and ten thousand pounds," he said. "You owe me that money. You will pay me." He slapped a piece of paper on the table.

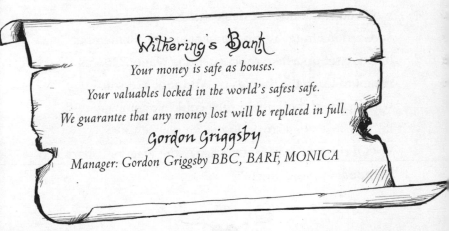

Withering's Bank
Your money is safe as houses.
Your valuables locked in the world's safest safe.
We guarantee that any money lost will be replaced in full.

Gordon Griggsby

Manager: Gordon Griggsby BBC, BARF, MONICA

"We didn't lose it," Griggsby said sourly. "It was stolen by an evil gang."

"It was stolen from your *thief-proof* safe," Silas Sharkle said and bared his teeth.

"It was stolen by your daughter," Griggsby said. "And I would not be surprised if you didn't put her up to it."

"You cannot prove that," Sharkle snarled.

Griggsby spread his hands. "I don't have to. We don't have your friend Preed – the one you sent to get the key – and we don't have the little gang your daughter worked with. But, we do have your daughter. Caught in the act!"

Inspector Beadle leaned forward. "Caught red-handed you could say!" He laughed till his bellies wobbled and made the desk shake.

Gordon Griggsby gave a faint smile. "Remember how we set up a fake robbery of the wagon? It was meant to teach the thieves of Wildpool a lesson – it was meant to show them they couldn't get away with it."

"Of course I remember. I drove the wagon," Sharkle snapped.

"Then we will give the thieves another lesson," Gordon Griggsby said softly. "We will hang young Charlotte in front of Darlham Gaol and show those thieves what happens when they try to break into the bank."

"That's not fair!" Charlotte cried. "I was only doing what I was told. . ."

"Hush, Lottie," her father said quickly. "You were only playing a game, weren't you?"

Charlotte pouted. "If you say so, Papa."

"I think I can see a way out of this," Inspector Beadle said. All eyes turned to him. "Mr Griggsby has been taught an important lesson. The thieves have done him a favour – they have shown him a weakness he didn't know about."

"I am not paying over a hundred thousand pounds for that lesson," Griggsby snorted.

Inspector Beadle raised a hand. "Wait, let me finish. Now, Mr Sharkle plotted to steal his own money—"

"How dare you say that!" Sharkle roared. "You can't prove that."

Again the inspector raised a hand. "I don't have to. We have the thief here in front of us – your daughter,

189

caught by my trusty constables. A girl who steals that much money has to hang. It's the law."

"It's not fair," Charlotte wailed again.

Inspector Beadle ignored her. "What if Mr Sharkle's bank box was empty? What if Charlotte broke into the bank and stole exactly *nothing*, Mr Griggsby. Would you still want to see her hang?"

Griggsby's round eyes glittered behind his round glasses. Roundly. "No," he said.

Inspector Beadle stared hard at Silas Sharkle. "So, Mr Sharkle. How much did you have in Withering's safe?"

Sharkle's jaw moved from side to side so his beard moved like a brush. He breathed as harshly as a pig at a trough. Finally he whispered, "Nothing."

"And how much money do you want from Withering's bank?"

Sharkle swallowed hard. "Nothing."

Inspector Beadle turned to Gordon Griggsby. "Charlotte Sharkle broke into your bank and stole . . . *nothing*."

"She damaged the floorboards!" Griggsby grumbled. "Someone can pay for that."

"Charlotte can pay," Sharkle snarled.

"I haven't any money, Papa!" the girl said.

"We'll sell your dolls' house," he told her.

"Oh," she sniffed. Then she got a cunning look in her eye. "I can tell you who helped me – give you their names and tell you where to find them."

Inspector Beadle shook his massive head. "There is no point. Nothing was stolen. Mr Griggsby does not want the police to charge anyone, do you Mr Griggsby?"

"I don't," the bank manager agreed.

Inspector Beadle rose to his feet. "So, that's it. Charlotte is free to go. The case is closed."

Gordon Griggsby smiled.

Silas Sharkle glared. He marched out of Wildpool police station and a girl in a red dress ran after him crying, "I suppose a golden dolls' palace is out of the question?"

He didn't reply.

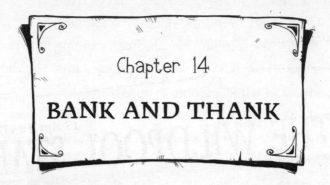

Chapter 14

BANK AND THANK

Tuesday 18th April 1837

The pupils of Master Crook's Crime Academy stood
at the window of their classroom and looked down
on the High Street. They watched Silas Sharkle march
from the police station towards the railway station.

He pushed past shoppers, he barged past the
stalls where shopkeepers showed their clothes and
vegetables, meat and fruit, boots and books, he
stamped through puddles and splashed the poor blind
beggar on the corner.

He brushed away the newspaper seller who was
selling the *Wildpool Star.* He didn't want to read the
news.

And he definitely wouldn't want to read the news the next day.

Wednesday 19th April 1837

THE WILDPOOL STAR

19 April 1837

CONSTABLE CLOWNS

On Monday night a daring attempt was made to raid Withering's bank on its first day. Thieves tried to enter through the night safe. Manager Gordon Griggsby told our reporter, "Nothing was taken because the thief-proof safe is thief-proof. People can leave their money safe with us . . . in the safe . . . safely."

Our reporter saw Norman Craggs, the safe builder, arrive very early with a new sheet of shining steel. It looked like a floor for the safe. Gordon Griggsby said, "Don't be ridiculous. As if we'd build a safe without a floor."

Mayor Twistle said he was shocked to hear of the raid. His police constables were aware that an attempt was being made. However, by the time they reached the bank they were only able to arrest a girl in a red dress.

"The constable clowns were at the docks when they were told to guard the bank," the mayor said angrily. "As soon as I see them I will rip off the medals I gave them earlier this month."

No arrests have been made. Inspector Beadle said, "The thieves probably came from Darlham. They escaped arrest by a whisker and got away with nothing. People of Wildpool can sleep easy. The bank robbers will not be back."

Smiff Smith looked out of the classroom window. He gave a sigh. "She won't be punished, then?" he asked.

"No," Alice said. "I never liked her, but I wouldn't want to see her hang."

"They don't hang rich people," Nancy muttered. "Only the poor."

A whistle sounded. It came from a speaking tube

that hung on the wall. Martin ran over and blew down it to show someone was answering. Then he placed it to his ear. He listened. He looked at the class.

"Master Crook wants to see us," he said. "Now."

The pupils followed Samuel Dreep down the stairs and into the basement. The room was dim, no windows and only a single candle. The pupils and the teacher sat on green wooden chairs and faced a curtain that hung across a corner of the room.

The curtain stirred as a door behind it opened. Master Crook did not step through the curtain. He never did. His deep voice rumbled through the room.

"Mr Dreep and I are sorry," he said.

Silence. Alice said, "What you sorry about?"

"Sorry we were fooled by Charlotte Sharkle . . . we let a spy into your class. And she set a trap that could have caught you all. I'm sorry."

"But it didn't work," Millie Mixly said. "We got away with it."

"How did you get away?" Master Crook sighed.

"Alice saved us," Smiff muttered.

"Exactly. The girl that Mr Dreep threw out of his class . . . the girl that saw Charlotte Sharkle for what

she truly is. We all owe Alice White a very large 'thank you'."

"Thanks, Alice," the pupils said.

"Oh stop it!" Alice cried. Even in the dim light of the candle the class could see her blushing. "The others would have done the same . . . wouldn't you? We're a team. We fight for each other. Look at rule eleven."

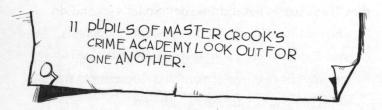

11 PUPILS OF MASTER CROOK'S CRIME ACADEMY LOOK OUT FOR ONE ANOTHER.

The class nodded silently.

"There are so many people out there who need our help," Alice cried. "We shouldn't be sitting here, moaning on about how we nearly got caught! We should be up in the classroom planning our next adventure. There are hundreds of rich people out there – people like the Sharkles – that make their money by stealing from other people. It's our job to get money to the right people!"

Her words rang off the walls of the basement room

and died into silence. "Erm . . . thank you, Alice . . . that is *exactly* why I set up this academy."

"And you didn't set it up so we could sit down here talking, did you?"

"No I—"

"No, you didn't. One day someone is going to ask us to tell the story of Master Crook's Crime Academy. They won't ask us, 'Hey, what did you *talk* about?' No, they'll ask us, 'What did you *do*?' So let's go and do it!"

You have to admit Nice was right! Here you are reading the adventures of the Master Crook's Crime Academy, just as she said . . . over 60 years ago. No one will ever raise a statue to Nice White . . . it's the rich villains that get the statues . . . but at least she and her friends are not forgotten. Not as long as you read her story. Nice says thank you!

The pupils jumped to their feet and ran to the door. "Come on, Mr Dreep, what are you waiting for?" Smiff laughed as he disappeared.

"Erm . . . class dismissed," Master Crook said.

"I think they already have," Dreep said faintly.

In Wildpool police station, Constables Liddle and Larch stood in their red-smudged uniforms. The little mayor, Sir Oswald Twistle, stood in front of them and ranted. "One hundred and ten thousand pounds," he shouted. "You stood there and watched some villains wheel away one hundred and ten thousand pounds in a barrow and did nothing."

"Sorry, sir, were we supposed to help them? It did look a bit heavy," Larch said.

"Yes, we should have helped," Liddle nodded.

"You should have *stopped* them . . . searched the barrow . . . saved Mr Sharkle's money!" the mayor raged.

"Inspector Beadle said nothing was stolen," Liddle argued.

"Yes . . . ah . . . yes . . . as far as the people of Wildpool know there was no money stolen. That's what Mr Sharkle and I are *saying*."

"So it's a lie then? You and Mr Sharkle are telling lies?"

"That's not the point!" the mayor snapped. "You let the thieves get away."

"With nothing," Larch pointed out.

"With . . . nothing," the mayor said. "But you should have stopped them!"

"Ah! But we were told not to touch the girls in the blue dresses," Larch said. "That was the message to Captain Hoo."

"Who?"

"Hoo!"

"I don't *know*," the mayor cried. "I'm asking *you*. But that is not the point. If *I* wore a blue dress would you let *me* walk out of this police station with a sack full of cash?" the mayor cried.

"No sir. If you wore a blue dress we'd lock you up! For your own good, of course. The whole town would laugh at you if we let you walk out on to the High Street in a dress," Liddle said.

"Have you got a blue dress?" Larch asked the mayor.

"No I have *not*!" Mayor Twistle roared.

"That's all right then," the policeman smiled.

Mayor Twistle reached up and snatched at the medals on the front of the constables' uniforms. He tore them off. "You are a disgrace to the uniform," he

said and stormed out of the door.

Liddle looked at Larch and sighed. "We're a disgrace to the uniform," he said.

"Yes but Mayor Twistle is a disgrace to the whole town!" Larch argued.

"How's that, Larch?"

"Coming in here, telling lies about money, and threatening to rob the police station wearing a blue dress. At least we're not as disgraceful as that."

"Very true, Larch, very true."

The two men wandered out into the sunny April morning. They breathed in the rotten air of Wildpool, looked up at the clouds as fluffy as dead sheep, and smiled. "Spring in the air," Larch said.

"Why should I?" Liddle asked.

The day after the robbery, Bunty McGurgle was tidying the money bags when she found a note that she had missed.

"There was a note with the money, Daddy!"

"Then read it, my little sweet-pea. Read it!"

Bunty, who always did as she was told, read it.

Dear Mr McGurgle,

Just before Mr Silas Sharkle's ship sank we managed to rescue some of the weapons. We sold them and made one hundred thousand pounds. Here is the money. Please do NOT sell weapons to China or anywhere else. They will only kill people.

Captain Hoo

P.S. Mr Sharkle doesn't know about this. Do not tell him or we will send a ship to take the money back.

Bunty McGurgle gasped. "That explains it . . . sort of. The main thing, Daddy, is we are not poor after all."

"No bailiffs!" Mr McGurgle happily cried.

"I was looking forward to a beef stew with those bay leafs," Bunty sighed.

"Oh, Bunty, you are a silly girl," her father said.

"I know. But at least I didn't lose a hundred thousand pounds," she shrugged.

LOOK OUT FOR MORE
MASTER CROOK'S CRIME ACADEMY
ADVENTURES!

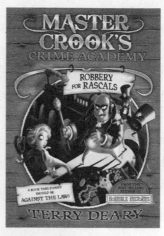